Hello…From the other side

(Bone chilling ghost tales by Travis D. Boothe)

Table of contents:

The sleepover

"Oh no!" Susan miller moaned as she looked at her alarm clock. "Why did I have to pick last night of all nights to forget to wind you?" She quickly sprang from bed and padded down the hallway, tying her robe around herself as she headed for her daughter's room.

"Megan, honey, you need to get up right now!" she called, but as she pushed the door open, she heard the sounds of Megan's shower running full blast.

Of course, she thought. *Not even a failed alarm clock could keep that girl from missing today out of school.* She shook her head as she caught a glimpse of the ghastly Halloween costume the girl had carefully laid out on her bed, a zombie princess. Wow, how times had changed since she was eleven, and girls wanted to be pretty things, like living princesses, mermaids, and fairies. She also knew that her daughter was far from the ordinary little girl. Megan was the kind of girl that tore the limbs from her dolls, read every book in the R.L. Stine *Fear Street* and *Goosebumps* series, and entertained herself with violent video games and movies, which would make Susan cover her face in fear from the opening sequence alone.

"See you downstairs in no less than fifteen minutes!" Susan screamed over the noise of the shower.

Her heart sped as she neared the bottom step. She smelled breakfast. Her senile mother was in the kitchen again. Luckily Susan had woken in time before the poor woman burned the house to the ground.

"Mom, we talked about this!" she said as she entered the kitchen. She tried to hide the annoyance in her voice. No doubt, the woman already felt virtually useless and embarrassed that her daughter and son-in-law had to move in to take care of her. The last thing she needed was to be scolded in her own home, but what was Susan to do? She couldn't have her mother operating the stove in her current mindset.

"How do you want your eggs?" her mother smiled, nodding her head towards a table that was full of pancakes, hash browns, sausage, bacon, muffins, eggs, and orange juice.

"I'm serious, Mother! You promised me that you wouldn't do this again." Susan sighed as she walked over and turned the burner of the stove off. She had lucked up this time. Today would be one of her mother's good days. At least she seemed coherent.

"Susan, I don't know why you make such a fuss. Really. I have been cooking breakfast my whole life. I may forget to take the keys out of the door sometimes, but the time to put me out to pasture has yet to come, my dear!"

"Mama, you know full well what Doctor McCloy said! We moved here to take care of you. You agreed to it. Why do you have to fight me every step of the way?"

"Well, isn't he the same doctor that told you that you would end up in a nursing home before I do, if you don't stop worrying yourself crazy over every little thing? Susan, I cooked breakfast! Look, the toast isn't even burned. Why are you making such a big deal out of it?" Loraine flashed her daughter a smile, which meant Susan would not be winning the argument today, as she piled pancakes on a plate and pulled a chair to the table.

"Alright," Susan shrugged, fixing a plate for Megan. "Truth is you're a lifesaver. I probably would have wound up sending my kid off with a glass of milk and a doughnut."

"It smells like IHOP in here!" Megan lamented as she entered the kitchen.

"Your mother really outdid herself today." Loraine gave Susan a subtle wink, and turned to address her granddaughter. "Aren't you the prettiest monster I've ever seen!"

"Pretty is not what I was going for…but thanks!" Megan was busy crunching on bacon as she spoke. "Mom, don't forget to pick up the supplies for the sleepover tonight, and please, whatever you do, don't forget to rent a copy of *Dorm Death 5*.

"You've seen that movie seven times already! Honestly, I don't know how you sat through it the first time. All the blood and gore gets to me. You definitely took your brave gene from your father's side." Susan chuckled. "Why don't we rent something you haven't seen?"

"Nope. *Dorm Death 5*," Megan insisted. "The fact that I already know all the scary parts is what's going to make it fun. The other girls haven't seen it yet. Can't you just imagine Terry's reaction when the slayer reaches through the toilet and pulls the girl's heart out of her chest? I swear; I have never met anyone as scary as Terry…except maybe Monica. If Monica even shows up tonight, I would be surprised."

"You promised to keep the invitations down to only five girls!" Susan reminded as she watched Megan cram the remainder of her pancakes into her fake-blood-stained mouth.

"Speaking of scary," Megan began, "Last night, I woke up to the feel of somebody stroking my hair. At first, I thought it was you or Dad, or maybe even Grandma, but then I remembered that I had locked my door, so it couldn't have been any of you guys."

"And you locked your door so that your father and I wouldn't know that you sat up half the night watching scary movies on your tablet," Susan shrugged. "Mystery solved. Maybe you felt the slayer from *Dorm Death* stroking your face, because you watched him right before bed. That explains your nightmare, now hand it over! We bought that as a learning tool, not for you to watch gore!"

Meghan knew better than to challenge her mother today. The last thing she needed was to be grounded on Halloween and have her well-planned sleepover called off. "It didn't feel like a dream," she tried to explain as she reached into her backpack and handed Susan the tablet. She gave up, knowing that her mother would only insist that that feeling of reality was indeed what made every nightmare so scary. Meghan was not the kind of kid who frightened easily or ever had nightmares, though. "Did Dad rig up the basement this year?" she asked with excitement.

"You know he did." Susan laughed. "I don't know which one of you kids is more excited about tonight, you or him. Too bad he can't be here to see you girls react to his little tricks and traps."

"Save a few of those for Danny, sweetheart," Loraine chided as her granddaughter reached for another helping of pancakes.

"Never mind. Just go to the bus stop." Susan sighed as Meghan flashed her questioning eyes.

Danny was Susan's long lost brother, the only person who loved Halloween more than her husband or daughter. Too bad neither of them got the chance to meet him. He had disappeared on Halloween seventeen years earlier, when Susan was twelve and he was fourteen. Susan never enjoyed the holiday the same, but she always did her best to accommodate her new family. Her daughter had never even heard mention of Danny until now, right when Susan was starting to convince herself that Loraine's senility was getting better.

"Mama, I have a really busy day ahead of me. I need you to go get dressed. We have to go to the store and pick out supplies for Meghan's party. Tonight is really special for her. Do me a favor, Ma; no more talk about Danny. I can't handle it today."

"You don't need me to come shopping with you, honey. Somebody has to stay here and keep an eye on your brother." Loraine was busy piling a plate up with the leftover breakfast as she smiled over her shoulder.

Is this a joke? Susan thought. *That has to be it. She hasn't forgiven me for taking away her driver's license, and now she is doing this whole "Danny" bit to get to me. Well, it won't work!*

Try as Susan may to pretend that mention of her brother did not bother her, she was scatter brained all day as she went through her list of chores. All she could do was recall the awful night he had disappeared, and the two days afterwards, when she sat alone in the parlor, in shock, unable to move, listening to the frantic adults, who had all seemed to forget she was there. Their focus was all on her missing brother while she was imprisoned in her own body, sitting in her own filth, her tiny hand clutching the glow in the dark ring he had given her from his trick or treat bag, promising her that it would keep her safe until he returned from hanging out with his friends.

When she had summoned the ability to scream out, she couldn't bring herself to stop, even when her parents finally came to show her some attention. That is when they took her away to a place filled with other children who screamed and cried all night, and doctors with cold eyes and long needles.

When she returned home, the truth became clear. Her life and family would never be the same again. This was made evident by her parents' constant bickering, the collection of empty liquor bottles that her father, who had never taken a drink in his life, had become custom of leaving scrolled around the house, and the crying fits that her mother carried on for over a year, before she finally decided to pack up all of Danny's belongings and move them to the cellar. The last to go was a huge portrait of him playing with their first dog, Dino. Whenever Susan's father had drunken himself unconscious, and her mother had taken enough prescribed medicine to allow her sleep, Susan would creep into the cellar and stare at the picture of Danny, lamenting over how much he looked like her father, before her father had started drinking, of course: the same piercing blue eyes and facial structure. The only difference was the huge, brown birthmark around Danny's left eye, and the cleft in his chin, the latter of which he had taken from their mother.

"Robert, this is your wife," she sighed into her phone, sinking deeper into the tub of bubbles. "You won't believe the day I have had. Please don't bail out on me tonight. I need you here, and even if you do decide not to come home tonight, at least call me and let me know. I at least need to hear your voice." Tears slid from the corner of her eyes as she washed down two sedatives with the last of her champagne. She had been well aware that Robert was living a double life for some time, but as long as he kept promises to Meghan, she was alright with keeping up the charade. After all, what other man would give up a home he had worked years for to move in and help care for his elderly mother-in-law?

Susan's train of thought was derailed as the sound of the fire alarm caused her heart to summersault in her chest. Not even bothering to towel off, she pulled on her robe and ran full speed into the kitchen, where her mother stood with a towel in hand, fanning a thick cloud of smoke towards the open window.

"It's okay, dear," Loraine promised. "I was making cookies, and I forgot about the last batch. Darn, and the peanut butter M&M ones were always your brother's favorite too. I guess he'll just have to settle for chocolate chip this year."

"Yeah, he will," Susan snapped, "because your time in this kitchen has come to an end! Go upstairs and watch your soaps, Ma. I don't want to hear anything else from you today…especially about Danny!"

"But, Susan, I'm trying to tell you--

"I mean it, Mama!" Susan knocked a pan of burned cookies to the ground as she yelled her last declaration. "Ma, I'm sorry," she whispered as she watched a look of shock and hurt distort her mother's face. She had never raised her voice to her mother a day in her life.

"It's alright." Loraine flashed a phony smile. "I'll get out of your hair, dear. If you need my help with anything, just call. I'm not as useless as you may think."

"Your mom makes the best meatballs!" Monica Richards exclaimed grabbing the last two off the tray.

The other girls were piled on Meghan's bed, huddled together in fear of the slayer, as *Dorm Death 5* blared from the big screen TV.

"Why did you have to invite her?" Crissy Monico whispered. "All she has done since she's gotten here is stuff her chubby face and play with your old dolls. I mean, you did tell her this was a Halloween gathering, right?"

"Some people don't like to be scared," Meghan sighed, thinking back to the look on her mother's face when she realized that Robert would not be coming home, leaving her in charge of operating the haunted house he had rigged in the basement.

Though tonight marked her first Halloween without her father, she had to admit that Susan's genuine screams of terror were more exciting and amusing than her father's fake chuckles and lackluster impersonation of Vincent Price as she lead the girl's through the rigged up basement. For what it was worth, her mother had gone out of her way to make this the best ever Halloween, even though everyone knew Susan hated the holiday.

"Shhh!" Ashley Minks chided as she and Terry Miller clung to one another for dear life. "I think he's about to …"

"AHHHH!!!!" All the girls besides Meghan screamed at once, before Ashley could even finish her statement.

"If you think that scene is bad, wait until you see what he does to the dorm monitor." Meghan shrugged and leaned over to scoop up a handful of popcorn.

"It gets worse?" Vanessa Lewter kept her eyes glued to the screen, nervously twisting a handful of her long braids as she spoke. "Your mom lets you watch this type of stuff all the time? My mother wouldn't even let me see *Hunger Games*, because she thought I would get nightmares."

"Meghan' mom is the coolest," Monica exclaimed from the corner of the room. "These cookies are the best ever!"

"You have to thank my grandma for those," Meghan giggled as Monica's comment caused the other girls to erupt with laughter. "My parents say she's getting senile…whatever that means, but she still can cook better than anyone I know."

"Well, in that case, I wish my grandmother was senile!" Monica joked, forcing more cookies into her full mouth.

Ashley glared over at the chubby girl with annoyance, and rolled her eyes. Just when she had opened her mouth to tell Monica what a downer she was being, a loud, collective scream from her other friends, caused her words to freeze in her throat before she was finally able to release a scream of her own. When she looked back at the television, the slayer was holding a beating heart in in his hand, raising it to his fang-filled mouth with a smile of satisfaction.

"No more for me!" declared Vanessa. "You ladies enjoy the rest of this bloodbath. I'm going to crawl into my sleeping bag and go to sleep, while everyone else is awake and I feel safe."

"Oh, come on!" whined Crissy. "There's still another hour and a half left! You're calling it quits on us after only fifteen minutes?"

"Everybody can't handle it." Once again, Meghan shrugged.

"Pause the movie," begged Terry. "I really gotta pee." She remained in her spot after Meghan had complied with her plea.

"Well," urged Ashley. "Are you going or not? Some of us actually want to find out how the movie ends!"

"Somebody come with me?" Terry trembled as she jumped up and down in need of relief.

"This is ridiculous!" laughed Meghan. "We haven't even gotten to the scene where he reaches through the toilet."

"On that note, I think I'll come with you," moaned Crissy, "and when I get back, I think I will follow Vanessa's lead, and call it a night. I have been scared enough for a lifetime already."

"Me too," Terry admitted. "I can't take any more of the slayer!"

"It's just you and me then, Ashley," Meghan giggled, restarting the movie.

"Never mind." Ashley rose from the bed and headed towards her sleeping bag. "It's not the same without everyone."

Meghan laughed to herself, knowing that Ashley was probably more afraid than any of the other girls. At least she could give Monica credit for admitting from the beginning that she couldn't deal with blood and gore. The rest of the girls were completely ridiculous. "Best night ever!" she laughed as she cleared her bed of the junk food containers and climbed under the covers. "All good things have to end though, don't they?"

"I had a blast!" Monica spoke for the first time without food distorting her words. "Meghan, will you mind if I sleep with your Penny Glow Bright doll tonight? I left my bear at home."

"Have her, if you want." Meghan giggled. "I don't play with baby dolls anymore. My mom just won't stop buying them."

"Thank you!" Monica climbed into her sleeping bag and closed her eyes tight as she listened to the sounds of her giggling friends, returning from the bathroom.

"Okay, guys. Keep it down from now on," Chided Meghan. "Try not to wake my grandma. Mom says she's had a rough day."

The girls all agreed, and lie silently trembling in their own personal spaces as sleep overtook them.

Vanessa tossed in her sleep, pushing a handful of her braids from her face as images of the slayer from the movie flashed in and out of her dreams. The girl had always been a light sleeper and the sounds of her friends, who snored and farted close by was beginning to summon her from her slumber. She refused to give in to reality's call, not with everyone else in the house fast asleep. She decided to lie still and keep her eyes closed, until a creaking noise pierced through the snores and eerie silence. Her doe-like, brown eyes flew open on instinct, and her head turned in the direction of the noise, towards Meghan's bed. What she saw caused her heart to stop in its tracks, and then speed up again. Peering at her from under Meghan's bed was the face of a strange, unkempt man, his face covered in remnants of red liquids.

"Very funny, Mr. Miller." Vanessa was prepared to write the incident off as only another of Meghan's father's elaborate pranks, but then the look on the man's face told her a different story as he pulled the trap door closed and she listened to him scurry around in the basement below. She gathered her nerves enough to reach out and grab her cell phone. As she checked the time, she was confident that this had not been another of Mr. Miller's pranks. Not even a big kid like himself would disturb sleeping kids at 2:45 in the morning.

She scrambled to her feet, hugging her flannel pajamas close as she tiptoed closer to Meghan's bed and tried to shake the sleeping girl into consciousness.

"Wake up!" she begged, so nervous that her voice sounded as if she were standing before a rotating fan blade as she said them. "Damn it, Meghan, wake up!"

In a matter of minutes, Meghan was sitting up with annoyance as she rubbed at her eyes. "What the hell, Vanessa?"

"Somebody is in your house," the visibly shaken girl exclaimed, just above a whisper. "I saw him come up through a trap door under your bed. He looked me right in the eyes, and then…"

"Halloween is over, V.!" Meghan pulled her blanket closer to herself and rolled over. "Why don't you try that with Monica? I'm sure you can get her to pee a little for you!"

"Goddamn, you!" Vanessa angrily snatched the covers from Meghan and seized her arms. "I am telling you the truth! You continue to lie there if you want, but I am getting the hell out of here. The blood of these other girls is on your hands if you don't believe me!"

"Okay…okay!" Meghan gulped with fear as she realized the urgency on Vanessa's face and in her voice. She had seen the girl in many school plays, and she was certain that Vanessa was not capable of that caliber of acting. "You wake the other girls, and I will go get my mom!"

"NO!!!" Vanessa crossed her legs over and over, trying to hold back her desire to pee. "Meghan, don't leave me here; he saw me!"

"Alright, then you wake my mom and you tell her, while I get these girls up."

Vanessa weighed her options, and then decided that since, Mrs. Miller's door was just beside the bathroom, which she needed so badly, waking the woman, after she took a quick tinkle, of course, would prove to be the better option. She ran through the hallway, into the bathroom, where she quickly handled her business, not even bothering to wash her hands. Soon, she was outside of Susan's door, knocking only loudly enough to rouse the woman from her slumber, but hopefully, not alert the intruder.

"What on God's green Earth?!" Susan flung the door open in anger, still groggy from the earlier wine and sedatives. Her eyes would barely focused as the frantic girl before her tugged at her arm.

"Somebody was in Meghan's room!!!!"

"What?! Damn it, I told her that movie would get to the rest of you girls, and now look!"

"NO!" Vanessa struggled to keep her voice down, and put her finger up to her lips, signaling for Susan to do the same. "It wasn't a nightmare. I saw him. I wasn't sleep. He came up through a door under Meghan's bed, and he peered right into my eyes!"

Those words caused Susan's heart to leap into her throat. Not even Meghan knew that her bed sat over a trapdoor, which led to the basement. Susan and Robert had decided to purposely hide that tidbit from the curious preteen upon moving there a few months earlier, when Susan had rediscovered it and had reminisced over all the mischief that she and her older brother would get into by using that door to sneak into the basement when her mother was preoccupied. As far as Meghan knew, only a shabby, area rug existed beneath her bed.

"Listen to me," She caught Vanessa's trembling, brown hands between her own, using her motherly body language to apologize for not believing the child in the first place. "You head downstairs and wait for me by the door. I'm getting mother and the other girls."

"We're already up!" Ashley's voice came from behind. Susan turned to find the girls cuddled close together, Monica nervously clinging to a doll and a box of cookies as Ashley stared at her with disgust, and nervously twisted her long, brown hair.

Meghan stared at her mother with questions that fear and sleep deprivation would not let her voice. Sensing the urgency on her mother's face, she silently guided the other girls to the living room.

"Take the keys to the van off the hook, and I want you girls to lock yourselves in the car. Don't open it for anyone but me! Do you understand?"

Noticing that each girl still had a cell phone, Susan instructed them to call 911 as soon as they got to safety.

The girls nodded in unison, and carefully descended the steps, each peering down over the banister with each tiny movement, as if they expected something or someone from below to reach up and grab their feet.

Susan shuffled back into her bedroom, grabbing the knife she kept at her bedside in Robert's absence. As quickly as the sedatives and wine would allow her to move, she scrambled to her mother's door, and was delighted to find that, for the first time, Loraine had complied with her plea to leave her door unlocked in case of emergency. She put her finger to her mouth as Loraine's inquisitive eyes scanned the knife in her hand and then locked with her own.

"We have to get out of here, Mother!" she whispered in panic. "Someone has broken in. Grab your robe, and let's go. No questions!"

Loraine sprang from bed with the haste and agility of a woman less than half her age, and scurried into her robe and slippers. She froze, just as she was about to rush out and join her daughter.

"Mother, let's go!" Susan chided, wiping her red bangs from her face as the hair clung to a cold sweat.

"Oh dear. We can't leave without Danny!" Loraine tried to push past Susan as she called for her long-departed son over and over.

"That's enough!" Susan violently seized the frantic woman's shoulders and gave her a firm shake, which she instantly felt sorry for. "Mama, we have to get out of here."

"We can't leave Danny in here by himself!" Loraine continued to frantically plea as her daughter's grip tightened on her arm and she was pulled downstairs. "Sweetie, don't you remember that him being alone on Halloween all those years ago was how I lost him in the first place? We have to find him!"

Susan nearly froze, as she processed the fact that her mother actually remembered that Danny had gone missing. Adrenaline and concern for the girls caused her to continue dragging Loraine towards the front door, where they were met by two uniformed police officers.

The taller of the officers held his hands up, signaling for the ladies to remain silent. "We've talked to the girls, and we need for you two ladies to please join them outside, where it's safe," he whispered, smoothing his silky, black goatee over his handsome, brown face.

His redheaded partner silently ushered Loraine and Susan towards the driveway as Loraine carried on about Danny.

"Who is Danny?" asked the redheaded cop. "Is there someone else in the house?"

"Danny is…was my brother," Susan sighed with anger at having that nonsense take precedence over the current threat. She lit a cigarette, something she vowed to never do in front of her daughter, and brought it up to her lips for a quick drag. "He disappeared more than fourteen years ago. My mom never got over it."

"I'm sorry." The officer drew his weapon and entered the house behind his partner.

"Jesus!" Susan stomped out her cigarette as her eyes focused on the group of huddled girls. Her eyes narrowed in judgement as she noticed that Terry wore nothing more than a tank top and matching panties. "Does your mother think that this is appropriate attire for a sleepover?" She tried her best to push her judgement down and amp up her motherly instincts as she handed the trembling child her robe. Without speaking, she shot Meghan eyes that silently stated that she and Terry's friendship had just ended.

Meghan's eyes were focused on someone else. "No, Grandma! Don't!" she pleaded as she sprinted to subdue the old woman, who was making her way towards the entrance of the house.

"You don't understand!" Tears gushed from Loraine's eyes as she begged her granddaughter to loosen the hold on her waist. "Somebody has to save Danny! He's been lost and alone for so long, all because I wasn't there to protect him back then. I can't let that happen again. I won't!" With a swift elbow to Meghan's ribs,

Loraine freed herself and was preparing to enter the house again when a series of gunshots caused her to pause in fright. "Danny!" she blubbered as she swooned to the ground. "Poor Danny!!!"

Susan rushed to assist Meghan in composing the frantic woman, as the officers rushed from the house, busy talking on their radios, and calling in emergency and legal backup.

"We have two white males, one deceased upon arrival, the suspect wounded severely as we attempted to subdue him. He is hanging on for dear life, but I urge you to hurry the ambulance, and also send backup. This guy was amped up on pure adrenaline. Four shots to the torso before he even went down, and if you could see what he did to the poor other guys face you would…" The officer nervously smoothed his goatee as he peered over his shoulder noticing the distressed women in ear shout. "Just hurry."

Susan's mind ran as fast as her heartbeat as she processed the officer's words. Two white males? One deceased? Robert had left for work that morning while she was still in bed. No other male was supposed to be in the house, so who had the intruder killed? Could her mother have been right about Danny returning home after all of those years, and if so, would her mother always blame her for not believing her, and not saving his life? She shook her head, deciding that it was impossible, and that the wine and pills, along with the current chaos, was making her as senile as Loraine.

Pull your shit together for these kids, Susan! She plucked another cigarette butt to the ground as the paramedics rushed into the house with stretchers, trailing a line of four armed policemen.

"This shit can't be happening!" the darker of the first two officers wailed in disbelief. "WE left this guy upstairs, barely clinging to life! It's like he's from one of those slasher movies or something."

"Put down your weapon!" the officers began to encourage in unison. A series of shots followed, causing Susan to cuddle closer to her mother and the frightened girls. Tears ran down the faces of Vanessa, Terry, and Chrissy. A line of piss gushed from Monica's legs as she clung to the doll so tight that its inner lightbulb illuminated her chubby, frightened face. Ashley continued to twist her curly, brown hair in annoyance of the other girls' reaction. Like everything else in life that took longer than five minutes, and did not center on Ashley, the girl had quickly gotten "so over it." Meghan stared at the house as two bodies were brought out on stretchers. The look in her eyes was more intrigue than the fear that painted the faces of her family and peers.

"You don't want to see this, Ms.!" a short officer with a thick, Italian accent pleaded as Meghan watched her mother summon the strength to do something brave, something that involved gore, for the first time ever. "You really don't want to see this!" the officer begged as Susan peeled the sheet back.

A scream built in Susan's throat as she peered at what was left of her husband's once handsome face. Over half of it appeared to have been eaten off by a wild animal. No wonder he hadn't returned any of her calls, or bothered to make it to Meghan's party, an obligation that he never dodged. The poor guy had never even made it to work that morning.

Not wanting to call Meghan's attention to the situation, Susan held back her scream and her tears and made it over to the other stretcher.

"This one was eating the face off the other one when we came in," the gentle, dark officer placed his hand on Susan's shoulders, silently bracing her for the impending doom.

Quicker than she had brought herself to remove the other sheet, Susan quickly snatched the sheet from the other body, anxious to see what sort of person could be so heartless and wreck that kind of havoc on her husband. Poor Robert, literally never hurt a fly. No doubt, he had not even given the bastard under the sheets the fight he deserved. Robert was the type of man who barely even raised his voice.

"Goddamn you!" Susan shuttered as she stared into the face of the killer. Not even the sight of the bullet wound in his forehead could override her anger and cause the otherwise, easily rattled woman to look away from the cold eyes that stared lifelessly at her, still wide open, though the bastard was certainly dead. Glassy, blue eyes, Susan noted. She gathered her nerves and tilted the dead man's head to the other side, revealing a star-shaped birthmark around his left eye. Her body ran cold as she processed that her mother was right. Her brother, Danny had been there all along. She was now staring at his dead body after having come to grips with his death many years ago as a child.

"Danny!!!" Loraine approached the stretcher with fast, deliberate strides, wringing her hands and sobbing. "I told you Susan! I told you, and now look what you let happen to him, all because you didn't listen."

Susan pulled the sheet back over Danny's face as her mother's tears made all longing for the relationship that she once had with her brother, and all grief of losing him for a second time, vanish. All she could think about now was the fact that her husband was dead at the hands of that psychopath, and that Meghan was now without a father. "How long has he been in this goddamn house?" she asked, turning to her mother with rage.

Loraine covered her mouth with her age-spot ridden hand and stared at Susan in surprise of the anger. "Well dear, I told you, your brother has been here before you and Robert brought Meghan to stay! I told you over and over, but you wouldn't listen to me. When you said I couldn't live on my own anymore, I tried to tell you that you didn't have to disrupt your lives on my account; your brother was already here, taking good care of me, and now…" Loraine fell to her knees with tears.

"You bitch!!!!" For the first time, Susan looked at her mother with eyes that did not contain pity. Hatred poured from every pore of her body as she reached into her stockings, removing the knife she had stored on the way out. "You bitch!!!! Because of you, Robert is dead!"

"Danny is dead too, dear, or don't you even care about your brother?"

"Drop the weapon!!!!" the officers circled around Susan, shouting their request.

"No, Mama; don't!!!" Meghan pleaded, attempting to make her way towards Susan. An officer wrapped his arms around the bucking girl, grabbing her back from harm way as Susan continued to descend upon Loraine with the large knife drawn.

"Drop it!" That was the last order before three shots rang out, bringing Susan to her knees. The knife slid from her hand as she toppled over into Loraine's lap.

"You…sick…bitch!" After laboring to deliver those words, Susan's body froze in death, her eyes locked with Loraine's still radiating hatred.

"Grandma!" Meghan ran to the old woman with tears on her blushed face. For the first time ever, something had frightened the child. "Grandma!" she repeated, as her cold body vibrated with terror.

Loraine carefully let Susan fall to the ground as she stood to console her grandchild. "Grandma is going to take good care of you. Don't worry about a thing." She covered the girl's eyes as the officers placed a sheet over Susan's body. "Now that this mess is all over with, why don't you let Grandma take you in to warm up and fix you some hot apple cider and rainbow cookies? That was your Uncle Danny's favorite. Did your mother ever tell you about your uncle, and how smart and brave he was?"

"No," Meghan looked back at her friends, who had all begun to pile into Vanessa's mother's van, and she secretly wished that she could go along with them, forever, but Grandma had given her an order to come inside, and she had seen what happened all because nobody listened to grandma.

A Pile of Leaves

Angel Torres cringed at the sound of his mother's voice outside his bedroom door. He had escaped the calling of a new day's duties three times that morning, first by cutting the snooze button on his alarm clock on twice, and finally pulling the blaring siren from the socket. Unfortunately, there was no way to turn his mother off, though he often wished escaping her high-pitched, nasally voice could be so simple.

"I'm up!" he whined, throwing his long legs over the side of the top bunk and jumping to the floor. He was glad that she had walked away from the door before she could see him take the quick route from the bed, and therefore, he didn't have to hear her drawl on and on about medical bills and his carelessness.

He cussed to himself as he realized that his younger brothers had beaten him to both bathrooms, thanks to his hankering for extra sleep. He looked around the room for an empty cup, a bottle, anything that he could relieve the urgency of his bladder into. When he saw that the room had already been cleaned of all such things, he frowned and darted to the balcony at the back of the house. Hopefully, the nosey neighbors on both sides would still be asleep, and they would not catch a glimpse of him pissing through the rails of the balcony, and onto their meticulously kept gardens.

Times like these made him crave the old apartment he and his brothers had shared with his mother and father in the slums of Hell's Kitchen, where pissing off the balcony was not only acceptable, but encouraged by the perverted onlookers, and could also give you a good laugh if your aim was good enough to wake one of the drunken, sleeping bums.

He didn't understand why he was made to leave everything and everyone he had grown up with just because his father had died, and his mother no longer felt safe in her own neighborhood. Even though she had blamed the move to Florida on her concern for their safety, Angel had not begun to feel unsafe, out of place, or uncomfortable up until the move.

"Goddamn it!" The angry voice of his next door neighbor boomed like thunder after the first few drops were relieved. Angel opened his sleepy eyes wider and peered down to see the old man looking around frantically, trying to find the source of the pissy assault. Angel managed to zip his pajamas and duck back into his house before the man's evil eyes could get a glimpse of him.

Though he still had to pee, having cut his earlier relief short, he thanked God that disaster had been avoided, and that his mother would never know that it had been his piss that had sent the poor, old bastard into such a frenzy. With the school's Halloween dance just around the corner, the last thing he needed was to be grounded, and to miss out on the chance to have normal socialization with his new peers outside of school.

All though he couldn't deny that he loved the new house ten times better than the two bedroom apartment that his family had left behind, he couldn't help but miss playing with his friends from the old neighborhood. No kids, especially not in his age range, lived close enough to allow him and his brothers visits to their houses.

His mother had called the neighborhood a retirement spot, which meant that, besides her, everyone else who lived there was too old to have young children. Since his mother was strict, and did not allow her kids to travel outside of the fenced in yard without her supervision, Angel had to make an easy choice between hanging with his two brothers, Anthony, age nine, and Cordell, age eleven, or staying in his bedroom all day, and entertaining himself with video games. Being nearly fifteen, he obviously opted for the latter choice.

"What did you do?" Cordell asked, staring at his older brother with accusing eyes as he slipped a pair of underwear on beneath the towel around his waist. "You did something. It had to have been you! Anthony is still in the other bathroom, and I just came out of this one, so why is Mr. Forell downstairs yelling at Mom?"

Angel shrugged, and pushed past his brother as he said, "We don't have to do anything for people like him to make a big deal about us living here. Do you see anybody else in this neighborhood that looks like us?"

Cordell rolled his eyes, remembering all the times that Angel had played the race card to get him out of trouble since moving to the new neighborhood. The truth, as far as Cordell could see, was that the elderly, white neighbors were nice people, who had earned the right to quiet and peace in their last years. They often smiled and waved at him and his brothers as they walked past, and sometimes brought baked goods and trinkets to their mother. That was before Angel had started to terrorize their pets and wreak havoc on their property. Though Cordell and Anthony both knew the truth, they had to lie for their older brother, trying to escape the threat of being beaten to a bloody pulp by him, as they listened to their mother blindly make one excuse after the other for Angel's antics.

"You will just have to ignore it, and remember what I told you about there being good people and bad people of all colors in the world," their mother would remind Angel, wiping fake tears from his eyes with each accusation from a neighbor. "Since they want to make it hard for us to live around here, you be on your best behavior. It's now your job to make it that much harder for them to hate you!"

"Ms. Torres, do you own a dog?" Steven Forell was now talking in his calm voice, though he could still be heard all over the neighborhood. "A huge cat, perhaps?"

"No, and it's **Mrs.** Torres. My husband is dead, but I was married, despite what you may think!"

"I don't care about…" Steven placed his hand over his chest and took three deep breaths. "***MRS. TORRES***, unless you have a pet, or a ghost, who drinks too much soda, I have to assure you that one of your sons pissed off your balcony and unto my lawn, hitting me as I weeded my garden!"

"Did you see them do it?" Angela stared at Steven with mutual anger, recalling that this had been the fifth time of the week that he had come to her door, accusing her children of mischievous acts, which all denied with innocent faces and teary eyes.

"I am warning you, you'd better…"

"I'd better what?" Angela raised the empty skillet over her head, trying to look as threatening as possible, though she had literally never even swatted a fly in her forty two years of living.

"This is a retirement neighborhood, **MRS.** Torres. Maybe this is just not the place for you and three unruly boys!"

"How dare you!" Angela was about to follow Steven off the porch when the sounds of her sons coming into the living room stopped her in her tracks. She sighed and tried to clear her face of anger as she closed the door and spun around to address the two younger boys. "Eggs and toasts are already on the table."

"What was he mad about?" Cordell pried, knowing that his mother often tried to hide every problem from them.

"Don't even worry about it!" Angela began to hum the gospel song her grandmother had taught her as a child while she scrubbed away at the already clean cabinet. "Where is your big brother?"

"Upstairs, in the shower. Me and Anthony just got out." Cordell hoped that his words would make his mother's brain leap to the same conclusion his had reached, that if he and Anthony were both in the bathrooms, the culprit of the mysterious offense had to be Angel.

"Of course!" Angela sighed as she took off her rubber gloves. "You boys were both in the showers, and now Angel is in the shower. So who could have pissed on Forrell's garden? I don't know, but it certainly couldn't have been either of my kids, huh?" Angela lit a cigarette and stepped to the open window. She wished her husband was there to make raising three boys, and also dealing with the hateful neighbors, a lot easier. She was always the quiet one in their union, but she no longer had that option, not if she wanted to ensure that her children did not get pushed around, as she had been all of her life, just because of skin color and origin. She had to be the fighter now, and even though doing so made her a nervous wreck, she would continue for as long as she had to.

"Hey, Mom!" Angel gave his mom a cunning smile as he leaned in and kissed her on the cheek. His hair still dripped from his quick shower, splatting her cigarette. She secretly thanked God for that happening, since that had been her fourth one since awaking two hours earlier. She couldn't explain it, but it seemed as if God had begun to use her kids to send her messages, especially the eldest. To her, her son had become just his namesake, an angel.

"You're running late." Angela smiled back at her son and ran her hands through his damp hair. "Just for this morning, forget the breakfast on the table. Grab a couple of toaster pastries and eat them as you walk your brothers to the bus stop."

"Okay!" Angel looked at his brothers and flashed them a menacing grin as he relished in the fact that he got sugar for breakfast while they scoffed down scrambled eggs and toasts. "Come on, Dumb and Dumber!"

"Don't tease them, Angel!" Angela whined. "And don't say anything besides good morning to Mr. Forell; I mean that! I won't have them saying that I didn't teach my kids manners. He's in his ways again today, but you let me handle that. You just say 'good morning,' and keep going to the bus stop! I mean it!"

"Again, this morning?" Angel tried to look innocent as he stared into his mother's glossy eyes. "What did he accuse us of this time?"

"That doesn't matter." Angela rose from her seat and stood on her tiptoes to kiss Angel's forehead. She smiled to herself as she thought of how strange it was to have to do so, when just a year ago, he was the same height as her nine year old son, Anthony. Her usual smile had returned as she bent to kiss Anthony and Cordell on the cheeks. "Be good!" she called behind them as they ran through the fence and towards the bus stop.

"Keep walking!" Angel warned his brothers as he noticed the hate-filled glare in Steven Forrell's eyes.

The man looked away as the kids approached, and continued to mumble to himself as he labored with raking the bountiful supply of fallen leaves in his otherwise, well- kept yard. So far, he had managed to arrange all of the leaves, beside the loose bunch he still fussed over, into three neat piles, all ready to be bagged and taken away before the boys could return from school.

"Hi, Mr. Forell!" Anthony called, giving the old man his usual smile and wave. Despite what his brother had tricked his mother into believing about Steven Foller, Anthony, like Cordell, still saw him as the nice man who had given them candy and other treats, and had made common practice of telling him and Cordell intriguing stories of his experience in two different wars while they played outside.

"Hello, boys!" Steven was too mad to smile and wave, but too good natured to ignore a greeting from two good kids. He rolled his eyes as their older brother drew close.

"Hey, Foller!" Unlike his younger brothers' greeting, Angel's tone was mocking, and tinted with adolescent arrogance.

"Don't you own a belt?" Steven rolled his eyes as the sight of the boy's low hanging jeans. "Jesus, when do they start to not care about appearance?" he questioned aloud, as he made note of the contrast between Angel and his well put together siblings.

"What's the matter, Forell? Scared the other neighbors might catch you sneaking a peek?" Angel pulled his boxers down as low as his pants had been hanging, revealing his bare ass to the already peeved man as he rushed by.

"One day, you're going to make me forget that you're just a snotty, little child!" Forell warned, turning his head in disgust. He was too busy trying to get the last of the leaves into his neat pile to notice that Angel had doubled back, crossing behind him to kick the other three piles over. Only the teen's clumsy footsteps aroused his suspicion. "You goddamn punk!" he squalled, throwing the rake down to give chase. "Today is the day I forget you are a child, you bastard! Come back here, and you take this ass whipping!"

Angel laughed as he encouraged his brothers to run faster and ignore the crazy, old coot. His dark eyes sparkled with delight as he peered over his shoulder, noticing that they were at least a block ahead of Forell.

Finally the old man gave up on the chase and headed back towards his own house, clutching his chest as he labored for air. "I will not forget this!" he screamed one final time.

"Are you going to ask her today?" Angel's closest friend Todd, pushed his wiry dreadlocks from his face and wiped sweat from his brow with his t-shirt. He used his head to motion to the short, brunette, Carla Lessinger. Though Angel tried to make himself believe that only he and Todd knew of his secret crush, his feelings for the older girl were well known, and often joked about amongst his peers. "There is only one week left before the dance!" Todd encouraged.

"Maybe." Angel smiled to himself, thinking that he was lucky enough to be the only freshmen in tenth grade honors English, a class he shared with Carla. He decided that he could wait until the next period to pass her a note rather than ask her in front of a gym full of boys his age, all waiting to laugh if she rejected him.

"You know what they say about he who waits." Todd gave another smile as he patted Angel on the back and threw his heavy backpack on his shoulder.

"I'll remember that." Angel smiled back and headed in the opposite direction. He couldn't explain why, but for some reason, he couldn't shake the sickening feeling that something was off today, totally wrong. Even though he and Todd had not been caught sharing their usual cigarette in gym, he had breezed through a math test, and he had gotten the best of Foller before school, something didn't feel right in his adolescent soul. It wasn't just his nervousness over finally talking to Carla either. Something *really* was off.

Just as with his other classes of the day, he filed into Honors English, trying to maintain his machismo. He couldn't bring himself to make his usual jokes or anecdotes, which the teacher, as well as the students, would all delight in, because the teacher was thrilled that a kid so young knew of the archetypes and pop references he played on, yet again, rewarding Angel's bad behavior.

All though Greek Mythology had been one of his biggest interests, since he was eight years old, he couldn't even bring himself to showcase his vast knowledge and understanding of *The Trojan War*, which usually caused his older classmates to shrink into their seats, angry that the youngest member of the class had shown them up once again.

Something was way off today, but what?

His heartbeat sped as a student helper handed Mr. Horton, the English teacher, a note from the office. He began to think that maybe he and Todd had not been so lucky or inconspicuous with their smoking after all. More and more frightening thoughts ran through his mind as he watched Horton's face grow grim after reading the note.

"May I see you out in the hall for a moment, Ms. Lessinger?" The teacher motioned towards Carla, who pushed her long brown curls from her face, and stared in shock.

Even after finding that the note was not for him, Angel's anxiety did not subside. Something was definitely wrong. Carla was one of the school's top students, editor of the school paper, a member of the debate team, student counsel, cheerleading team, and math team. She never got in trouble. What could the note have said?

Angel's curiosity was peeked further as he heard the girl let out a loud cry. Moments later, she returned, teary eyed, and gathered her books.

Class went on for the next forty-five minutes, but Angel's mind was absent, wondering what the note had said. What was so important that it couldn't wait less than an hour for the girl to return from school? He also wondered if the obviously disturbing news would keep Carla out of school for the next week, causing him to miss his chance of asking her to the dance. He felt a little guilty that that selfish question outweighed the others in his mind.

After school, he walked two blocks over to meet his younger brothers, and they caught the only bus that ran through their neighborhood home. Antwon and Cordell chatted on and on about what they had learned in school, and also about what girls they liked or thought liked them, but angel stared out of the bus window, quiet for the first time ever. His already occupied mind went into overdrive as the bus neared their stop, and he noticed that his mother waited for them, a cigarette in her trembling hand.

Forgetting that it was his job, as the older brother, to see his younger siblings safely off the bus, he leapt from his seat and ran to the entrance. "What the hell is going on?" he asked before the door could even open completely. When his eyes locked with his mother's he repeated the question with more tact, "What's happening, Ma?"

Angela tried to smile, but it was obvious that she was a bundle of nerves. "There's been a death," she said softly, leaving the boys to wonder who had passed and why she was so sad. The four of them were all that either had left of family.

"Who died?" Anthony beat his brothers to the punch.

"Forell," Angela wept, as if she and the man she argued with every day and night were lifetime friends. "His wife went to check on him, after he didn't come in from raking the yard, and she found him, face down on a pile of leaves. They think he had a heart attack."

"Wow!" Angel's throat clamped shut as his mother ushered them past the busy street, lined with cars of people who had come to pay respect to Forell's widow. He wondered if he were responsible for the old man's death. After all, he had made the poor cot give chase to him for nearly three blocks. Though he would never admit it, he was glad that his mother was there to wrap her arms around him and his brothers as they passed Forell's yard, still decorated with the scattered piles of leaves Angel had kicked over that morning.

As they walked, his eyes caught a glimpse of Carla Lessinger. She sat on Forell's porch, bawling her eyes out as Mrs. Forell sat beside her on the porch swing, one arm around the crying girl as she stared off, her own glassy eyes looking vacant.

"Apparently, that is their granddaughter," Angela informed, noticing Angel's interest in the scene. "Do you know her?"

"Yeah. We have honors English together."

"Maybe you should go over and see if you can cheer her up," his mother suggested. "I bet she would be happy to see a friend from school, someone who can take her mind off of all of this. Who better than you, after what you just went through with your father?"

"NO!" Angel's voice cracked at the thought of stepping one foot on Forell's lawn, even if not doing so meant he missed the perfect chance to talk to his secret crush in private. "She needs to be alone with her family." He bolted past the part of the lawn that was joined with the Follers' and ran upstairs to his room, where he spent half the evening staring out of the window, watching the leaves blow around the neighbor's yard.

"It's eleven o'clock!" Angela chided as she passed the room Angel shared with Cordell. "You two turn that video game off now! I don't care if tomorrow isn't a school day."

"Okay." Cordell agreed, already sleepy, but so happy that his older brother had finally let him touch the extra game controller that he couldn't pass up the chance.

"Just let me save this part of the game to the memory card!" Angel begged.

"If you can't do it in three minutes, it's lost forever!" Angela warned, turning down the hall to check on Anthony. "I mean it! Don't test me tonight you don't know the kind of day I have had!"

Angel sulked to himself as he turned the game system off, and then headed to the open window. Why did he, at nearly fifteen years of age, have to abide his mother's strict schedule, only so that his baby brothers wouldn't feel jealous? Not being able to venture outside of the yard's fence because Cordell and Anthony had no sense of direction and couldn't fight their ways out of a paper bag, was bad enough, but having to turn off his one means of escapism, in the confinement of his own bedroom, was just taking it too far.

"When will she finally learn to let me go?" He sighed as he struggled to pull the stuck window down. He briefly turned his head, preparing to ask his brother to aid him in the task, but he turned his attention back, after noticing that Cordell was already asleep.

As he tried to force the stubborn window shut, his eyes locked on something moving beneath in Forell's yard. It was a pile of leaves, at first. The more he stared, the more the movement of the leaves, and even the shape, became that of a human. He rubbed his eyes, noticing that the leaf-person seemed to walk closer and closer to the side of the yard that his window faced.

"It can't …b…be!" he stammered, unable to turn and run from the frightening sight. Just as the pile of leaves became unmistakably human in form, Forell's form, to be exact, the sound of his mother turning off the light outside his door caused him to look away.

"What are you doing by that window?" Angela asked, stopping again to check on her sons. "Angel, what did I say I would do to you if I caught you smoking again?!"

"I…I…wasn't!" Still frozen in fear, Angel looked back and forth from the window to his mother. He wanted to be relieved that the humanoid pile of compost had returned to its usual state, but that only meant that Forell was being insidious, waiting for a chance when Angela and the other boys were not around to witness before he took his revenge. "Do you have a few minutes?" he asked his mother. "I really want to talk to you about something."

"What is it, Bunny?"

Angel tried not to show his annoyance at mention of his childhood name. He had long grown into his oversized front teeth, and had switched from glasses to contacts upon starting high school, which meant that his eyes didn't seem to pultrude. Still, he was glad that his mother was there with him at that point in time. The truth was, he had nothing to talk to her about, but, how would it seem to her if he revealed the truth, that he was afraid to venture across the hall to the bathroom, and needed her standing at his doorway to make the trip feel safer? Even worse, she would be ready to cart him off to the funny farm, no doubt, if he told her that the leaves outside were possessed by Mr. Forell. But they were!

"I just got to grab a quick pee. Wait here, please?" he darted to the bathroom, thinking of what excuse he could make for requesting his mother's presence when he finally returned.

If I return, he thought to himself, as he noted that the bathroom window overlooked the same plot of ground beneath. He tried his best not to even cast his eyes out of the portal as his urine shot into the stool. He couldn't even find the nerve to keep his life-long habit of washing his hands once he had finished. Instead, he quickly turned off the light and all but ran towards his bedroom, his mother's presence was the only thing stopping him from being in full stride.

"What's the matter?" Angela caught the boy's arm as he attempted to race past her. "You look white as a sheet! Has what happened to Mr. Foller brought back memories of us losing your father? Is that what you wanted to talk to me about?"

"No. I'm fine." Angel didn't know why he chose to not take the easy route his mother had given him as he climbed into bed.

"Then what is this all about?"

"Nothing." He closed his eyes, telling himself that if he didn't watch her turn the light off, and if he didn't watch her walk away, he could get a full night's rest, fooling his young mind into believing that she would remain standing in his doorway, watching over him, as she had done many times when he was younger and sick.

"Dios Mio!" Angela cringed and wrapped her thick robe tighter around her. "What are you boys trying to do, catch your deaths, and run up two more doctor's bills for me in the process? This room is freezing! Why didn't you close the window?"

NO!!!!! Angel silently begged. *DON'T GO TO THE WINDOW!*

He instantly shot up in bed, and stared towards the window as his mother effortlessly pulled it shut with one arm. He wondered how that could be. He lifted weights three times a week, and outweighed his mother by nearly twenty pounds of muscle. The window was jammed just a few minutes before! He was unable to make it bulge while using both, muscular arms. How did she gently roll it down, as if it were on well-oiled coasters?

"What's the matter?" Angela asked, looking over her shoulder as she collected the plates and cups that her sons had left on the side of the room that was designated for homework. "And what is with all of these leaves everywhere?" She turned her attention to Angel as she scooped up a small stack of leaves from the floor. "Is it too much to ask for you boys to wipe your feet before coming into the house?"

"Sorry, Ma!" Angel tried to swallow the dry lump in his throat, but he was silently questioning how the leaves had gotten in the room, how many were already there, and how long it would take until they all transformed into Forell.

"Goodnight." Angela blew her son a kiss as she exited the room. "I'm going to be in my writing office, if you need anything."

Angel usually swelled with pride inside each time he heard that his mother had been, once again, bitten by the writing bug. He closed his eyes and recalled how she often laughed that she was a three times best-selling author, but was sure that the neighbors all figured that Angel was a drug dealer, and supported their lavish lifestyle, since none of them had asked her, and could not figure how she was able to afford such nice accommodations, let alone support herself and three sons while doing so. What else could they think, since none of them ever saw her go to work? Little could they all guess that the house had been brought with the stipend she had received from losing her teacher/firefighter husband to an out of control blaze two years prior. She kept food on the table and clothes on their backs by using her knack for words, a trait she had proudly passed down to all of her sons, especially Angel.

It's just a dream! Angel repeated that phrase to himself over and over as he watched himself walk out of his front lawn and cross over into Foller's leaf-filled lawn. *You can wake up, safe in your bed, at any time!*

All of the money his parents had paid for therapy when he had developed chronic bad dreams as a child was now paying off. He had learned to use several techniques, even when unconscious, to deal with the monsters and unresolved problems that plagued his mind at night.

One more step, and you'll be right there! He coached himself on as he watched the image of him walking towards Foller's porch, where Carla sat on the swing, tossing her long, Auburn hair over her shoulder. Her big, brown eyes locked on him, and a smile made her thick lips perch, showing dimples on the sides of her face.

If you can make it to the first step, you can forget all about crazy, old Mr. Foller forev...

"Stay the hell away from my granddaughter!" Foller's voice caused Angel to jerk around in his dream, coming face to face with Foller, who was covered from head to toe in leaves and dirt from the garden, where he had fallen while taking his last breath. His angry eyes were unmistakable as his hands reached out and wrapped around Angel's neck. Angel motioned for Carla to help, but she sat still, the same smile on her face, as her grandfather pulled Angel away from the porch by his throat. "Who's laughing now, you little punk?!"

"AHHHHHHHHHHH!!!!" Angel shot up in bed, covered in sweat. His heart thudded quickly against his chest while his eyes fought to adjust to the dim light of the room. His hair stood up on his arms, and his body shivered from the cold gust of wind coming in from the open window.

Wait! How did the window get open again?

He carefully leaned over the top bunk and looked around the floor, checking to see if Foller had already hidden himself somewhere in the room. His throat went dry as he noticed that the pile of leaves in the corner of the room had grown in size. A scream leapt from his throat as he saw it move, and he also heard the guttural sound of an angry, old man's groaning coming from the corner.

"What on earth?" Angela asked switching on the light to her sons' room. Angel had covered himself from head to toe with the blankets and trembled like a nervous rabbit. When she was able to pry the tightly tucked covers from under his head and feet, his eyes looked vacant and watery.

"What?" she asked again as he stared around the room and pointed to the once opened window, and where the large pile of leaves had just been. "Angel, what is going on with you?"

"I have to tell you something," he began, figuring that if Foller did pull off the inevitable, and took his chance to exact revenge upon him, his mother and younger brothers deserved to know why, especially since they could be in danger as well. "Promise me that you won't get mad."

"Sure." Angela gave her son the 'I'm only agreeing to this so I can figure out what your punishment should be as you talk' smile, and then sat at the edge of his bed. "I'm all ears."

Angela's face wrinkled with anger, as she listened to Angel recap the past morning's activities, along with several other horrible things he had done to annoy the Follers since moving in, things that Angela had defended him for tooth and nail, and had even found hatred in her heart for Foller over, when she had never hated anyone in her entire life.

"If you want to make these dreams go away, you have to make things right!" she told her son, "starting with marching your little ass over to Mrs. Foller's with me tomorrow, and you will volunteer to rake every single leaf from her yard while I sit with her and we talk over the cake I'm going to bring her"

'Will I have to tell her everything?"

Angela paused for a few seconds. She knew that saying no would send him the wrong message, but saying yes also put her in the hot chair, when she had been blind to his every act in the past. Neither she nor Mrs. Foller needed to think about all of those negative things at this time. "No, but you better make sure you get every single leaf! Foller, God rest his soul, kept an impeccable yard, and you owe it to him and his grieving wife, to make sure that it looks good during his funeral service! And long after then!"

"Really, Ma?!" Angel whined his disapproval, figuring that one act of kindness should have been enough to make up for everything he had done in the past, after all, nobody knew about those things besides himself, Foller, and his mother.

"That's the punishment! If you want to be man enough to look his widow in the eyes and apologize for *all* of the foul things you did, then maybe we can renegotiate."

"No."

"That's what I thought!" Angela fumed. "Lay yourself down, pray for forgiveness, and try to get some sleep. Tomorrow will be a busy day for you, mister!"

....

"Eat!" Angela urged as she watched Angel push his French toast around on his pate. His pussy eyes and re face showed signs that he had not gotten any sleep the night before.

"I'm not hungry." The boy pushed his favorite meal away and stared at his mother. "You're really making me do this?"

"Yes!" Angela's tone showed contempt for her son's selfish question. "I have the hard part! I have to look in that woman's face, thinking that you may have played some role in her husband's death, and I have to choke back secrets of all the crumby things you have done to him since moving here! All you have to do is rake a few leaves into a bag to ease your troubled conscience! Did you think about mine? Lord, angel! How many times did you make me cuss that poor man out, and call him a liar?!"

"I'm sorry!" Angel's voice came out a bit too aggressive, due to his lack of sleep. For the first time in his life, he actually did feel sorry about the things he had done to Foller, and the also for the many things he had done to other people in secrecy.

"Me too!" Angela fumed as her hand crashed against her son's face. "I'm sorry I didn't discipline you sooner. Grab your coat. We're going next door. Suit yourself, if you don't want to eat; you don't deserve a full belly anyway!"

"Can I trust you guys to not touch the stove or leave this house while we're away?" Angela asked her two youngest sons as she tugged Angel towards the door. Both agreed, all too eager to get their hands on the game system that Angel usually hogged away from them. "Okay. We will only be gone for a while, and you know how to knock on the neighbor's door, only if you need anything."

"Okay." They both agreed, waiting for the sound of the door closing before sprinting upstairs to boot the game.

"Hello," Mrs. Foller tried her best to sound her usual, upbeat self as she accepted the desert that Angela handed her, and then ushered the mother and son into her beautifully decorated home. "Please excuse the mess. I haven't felt much like cleaning since…"

"Of course, you haven't." Angela said, wondering where the mess was. As far as she could see, the Foller's home made her also well-kept house look like a pig's sty. "I didn't come to judge your house. I just wanted to give you the sock it to me cake I baked for you, and to give you my condolences." Angela pulled angel from behind her. "Speaking of keeping things neat, my son wanted to volunteer his services to your yard, for free, since you no longer have Mr. Foller around to keep things as beautiful as usual."

"What a sweet boy!" Mrs. Foller's face seemed to say the exact opposite of her words as she glanced at Angel. "The rake is in the back, where he left it."

"Yes ma'am." Angel quickly left the house, feeling as though Mrs. Foller had taken one glance at him and seen all of the hideous things he had done to her husband.

"Forget all about the stupid dreams!" he told himself as he walked to the back of the house. He chose to ignore the fact that he had not been asleep for two of the incidents. "Do this one simple thing, and it all ends, just like Mama said."

He stood completely still as a slight breeze caused the leaves to rustle and move around on the ground. After a few seconds, he laughed to himself, telling himself that he was only being crazy. Besides, Foller wouldn't…no…couldn't attack him in broad daylight, not with his mother right inside his house.

"I'm doing this to make amends." He said slightly beneath a whisper. "I'm sorry for everything I ever did to you; really, I am, but I'm just a dumb kid. Will you please let me alone, if I do this thing?"

Suddenly, a pile of leaves rushed towards him, causing him to jump back in shock and lose his footing. There was no wind blowing. Foller had refused his apology; he knew that for a fact, but he was also equally afraid to waltz inside and tell his mother that he refused to finish the yard, as he had promised.

"Please, man?!!!" tears gathered in the corners of his eyes as he picked himself up and grabbed the rake. Finally, the yard was still, giving him the courage he needed to breeze through three bags of leaves.

After a few more hours of labor, he looked over his shoulder and noticed that the sun had slid down in the sky. Evening was approaching and he did not want to be out there in darkness. He also didn't want to leave the job undone, which would only make him have to come back the next day.

"Jesus, be with me!" he moaned, as he crossed the yard for another trash bag.

The sound of rustling leaves caused him to stop in his tracks again, too afraid to look over his shoulder. Images of Foller's leaf-filled face danced through his head again. Tears mixed with the sweat that ran down his face.

"Hey!" The familiar voice belonged to Carla, but that wasn't enough to stop Angel from shuddering when her hand reached out and tapped his shoulder. "What is wrong with you?" She looked at him strangely as she handed him a glass of lemonade. "Grandma said you earned this. It's very hot out here. You know, we appreciate this, but you don't have to do this. Bob is coming by tomorrow. I can get him to finish. He likes to impress my mother and grandparents."

"Bob Wiskowsky?" Angel's face reddened at the mention of one of his biggest rivals, the twelfth grade heap of muscles, who was not only superb at sports, but twice as handsome as Angel, and also intelligent. "You really dating that loser?"

"Dating, no. Talking to, yes" Carla began to twirl her hair around her fingers as she stared at Angel. "What makes him a loser?"

"I don't know." Angel smiled, back, trying to turn on all the charms as he handed her back the empty glass. "Actually, he beat me to asking you out, so I guess he won."

"You were going to ask me out?"

"Too late to talk about it now." Angel stripped out of his sweat-soaked shirt, and turned away from Carla, trying to put into practice one of the rules his dad had taught him about girls, that if you act like you are not interested in then, their interest in you will increase.

"Why didn't you?" Carla walked around to face him.

"Why didn't I what?" He tried to act as if their conversation had already been forgotten.

"Doesn't matter now, huh?" Carla turned the game around and gave him one more smile before heading into the house.

Suddenly, the leaves began to fly around Angel, as if the neighborhood was experiencing a twister. He tried his best not to get spooked again as he turned his head to and fro, checking for a reasonable explanation. His heart didn't kick into overdrive until he realized that none of the other yards had been disturbed by the wind, and that he did not feel any breeze. "I'm trying to make it right!" he pleaded, still careful not to disturb the ladies inside the house.

Stay away from my granddaughter, you little shit!!!

Angel tried turned to run towards his own yard as the unmistakable voice of Foller bubbled through the rising leaves on the ground. A hand reached out and grabbed his leg, tripping him, and then pulling him backwards. When he regained the ability to scream, he still couldn't, because several leaves clung to his face, also arresting his ability to see or breathe.

I told you, I would get the last laugh; didn't I, punk?!!!"

More and more leaves covered Angel as he lay in a state of panic. All he could think was that it was impossible, especially since he had bagged all but a few. That was the last thought that crept through his mind, right before he was swallowed up by the pile of leaves, struggling and fighting so hard that two of his fingernails broke completely away from his fingers as he scratched at the ground, trying to gain leverage.

"Are you ready to go, Bunny?" Angela called, crossing to the back of the yard. "I let Mrs. Foller know that you would be back, if you…" Her words caught in her chest as she caught a glimpse of her son, lying face down on a pile of leaves.

"Angel!" she screamed, as she ran to shake him awake. "Wake up, baby! Please wake up!!!" she begged cradling his lifeless body, and smacking his face over and over.

Soon her sobs brought Mrs. Foller and Carla running out of the back door.

"Call 911!" Angela begged. "My baby isn't breathing!"

Mrs. Foller cocked her head to one side, noting that Angel had collapsed in the exact spot she had found her dead husband the day before. She decided to keep that observation silent, as she motioned for Carla to go make the call.

Angela!

Tears streamed down the frantic mother's face as she turned around, looking or the source of the male voice.

Angela, I warned you that his was not the neighborhood for three, wild boys!

"NO!!!!!" Angela screamed to the top of her lungs as she held her dead child close, and tried to shield her face from the barrage of brown leaves.

Mind over Matter

Vera Mai scooted herself up in bed, using her strong arms to make up for the lack of feeling in her lower extremities. Her sleepy eyes scanned the room for her wheelchair, which was normally kept right beside her bed, seeing as how she prided herself on being as independent as possible.

"Pai!" she called meekly, trying to summon her nephew, who always attended her while her sister and brother-in-law worked at the family's business, a crematorium, which existed just below the huge, five bedroom house that Vera's parents had willed her upon their death.

Her sister, Ping, being older, and having the use of all of her bodily functions, was the recipient of the crematorium. That decision, made by their dead parents, had caused jealousy between the once inseparable sisters, especially Ping, who saw Vera as a lazy ingrate, who got to enjoy the fruits of their parents' labor by pretending to be mentally and physically unable to care for herself. On the other hand, Vera felt a sting to her pride when she realized that their parents did not trust her to run the crematorium, even though it had been she who had sat up with her father during many nights of laborious bookkeeping while Ping danced at the clubs, dragging herself in just when Vera and her father were settling off to bed.

Unlike Ping, Vera did not voice her contempt, because she felt that her physical condition had already helped Ping win the argument.

"Not today!" Ping answered from the doorway. "Today, Pai not come, and Kim not come either. Today you stuck with Ping." Ping's smile widened almost as big as her sister's frightened eyes as she walked closer to the bed. "You get to tell me all the horrible lies you tell my son and my husband behind my back. Come on, Vera; tell Ping how awful she has been to you these years."

"I just need my chair," Vera winced as her sister approached. "I don't understand how it got all the way over there. Kim and Pai left it right here last night!" Vera waved her hand over the empty space beside her bed to mark her point.

"If you need your chair, get out of bed and get it." Ping sat on the edge of her sister's bed, gesturing towards the chair, which rested twenty feet away in a corner. If that distance hadn't been virtually impossible enough for Vera, the trip was made even more impractical by the fact the copper teapot, which had held her grandfather's ashes for most of their lives, was perched on a shelf in that very corner.

Following the loss of her best friend, a Yorkie Terroir, which Vera had named Sun, and had kept for three years, Vera began to suffer with plagues that would come and go with no explanation, save the one given by the five year old's doctor: Vera had discovered mortality, and being forced to deal with her own mortality, via the death of Sun, had caused the young girl to become a hypochondriac, thinking of new ways to die each time a placebo for the last illness arrived.

The one illness that had yet to mysteriously vanish as quickly as it had come was the paralysis to her lower extremities. At the age of eight, Vera woke up, unable to feel her legs. Her parents, and the family doctor, all gave the phenomenon the usual length of her other illnesses to run its course, but, two weeks later, Vera's legs were not working, though other false injuries continued to come and go as usual.

Twenty years later, Vera still could not explain why her legs had stopped working, nor could she make them work again. She, as her parents had also done before their deaths, had decided that she would never walk again. There was no need to keep looking for neither an explanation nor a cure.

Only one person dispelled the belief that Vera's paralysis was not indeed all in her mind, and that person now sat at the edge of her sister's bed, pointing to the teapot that contained the ashes of a man who had succumbed to tuberculosis and pneumonia.

Vera rolled her eyes as her heart beat with adrenaline. The mere thought of being so close to something that contained death and illness had tears sliding down her reddening face. Another illness that had developed later in Vera, but had stuck just as hard as the paralysis, was Mysophobia, the fear of germs. To Vera, Ping may as well have been asking her to crawl through broken glass, wade through a river of poisonous snakes, and eat the deadliest thing known to mankind. She had no doubt that her cruel sister was getting a kick out of watching her freak out. Ping, as she had explained to her nephew, Pai, and to her brother-in-law, Kim, was not trustworthy, and did not have a kind feeling left towards her own sister. Both men had promised to never leave her at Ping's mercy. Vera wondered just what Ping had done to gain this position.

"Pai not coming!" Ping raged, grabbing her sister by the shoulders. "Kim not coming! You want your chair; you go get your chair!"

Ping released her grip and allowed Vera to slouch back against her stack of pillows as she watched water fill her sister's eyes. "Can't, huh?" Ping's beautiful face reddened and her eyes swelled with anger. "That's the word you use every time something get scary to you, or seem too hard. Today, that word not work. You want your chair; you go get it!"

Vera's own anger roused as she watched Ping exit the room, mumbling to herself in their parent's native, Khmer tongue. She understood very well why Ping hated her. Who would blame her? While Ping was made to suffer as the only Cambodian student in a vastly white public school, Vera had the luxury of a private tutor to lecture her at home, which explained why Vera's English progressed much better than her sister's, seeing as how Ping became withdrawn, and ashamed to speak due to the taunts of her classmates.

Vera didn't see the point of being able to speak perfect English, when she had nobody to talk to but the walls most days. She considered Ping the lucky one, the one who got to attend prom, and got on dates with a barrage of handsome boys, all leading up to her finding Kim, someone who would be there for her in her time of sickness and old age. Ping would never have to depend on her sister's husband and child to help her through tasks that most people took for granted.

Vera stared at the teapot in the corner, wondering how Ping could be so mean as to honestly think she had willed herself sick. Who would want to go through pain, which a doctor could not cure? Who would trade romantic walks in the park with a loved one in order to have someone they could never love in a romantic way rub salve into their bedsores? Of course she longed to be normal, just as normal as Ping, bust she couldn't, and she didn't know how to make her sister understand that she was not being stubborn or lazy.

Vera's chest began to tighten as she stared at the teapot. Her breathing became suppressed, and she felt as if the room was spinning. Sweat began to pour from her skin as she labored to call her sister. "Please, Ping! Take the teapot out of here!"

"You move it yourself!" Ping's voice answered from the kitchen. "It bother you, not me! You get up and move it!"

Vera threw her torso over the side of the bed and began to vomit profusely. Everything went dark as her body toppled to the floor, sending her face down in her own vomit. When she awoke, unsure of how long she had been unconscious, she still remained face-down in her own puke.

"You finally decide to pick yourself up." Ping spoke from her seat at the room's door. "You smell like shit. You should bathe."

"Go fuck yourself!" Vera raged as she used her arms to scoot into a more comfortable position and mopped vomit away from her eyes with her hands. "If you aren't going to do anything to help me, at least give me my cellphone. I will call somebody who will."

"Who? Kim not coming! Pai not coming! You can help yourself, and you will help yourself! You have to, you stupid cow!"

Vera shook with tears as she thought back to the old Betty Davis and Joan Crawford movie she had watched many times since childhood. She and Ping had often acted out the famous, "You couldn't do these awful things to me if I wasn't in this chair," scene, but today that scenario did not amuse her, and she was sure that today would not end with Ping cuddling in bed with her and sharing candy.

"Why are you so angry?" Vera continued to weep as she etched further and further towards the chair in the corner, using her arms to pull her along, like a soldier crawling through brush.

"Nobody angry." Ping shook her head. "I can't help you! Don't I always, when I can? Damn you, I can't!"

"Then go away!" Vera stopped halfway and gave her sister her full attention. "Since you can't or won't help me, then why the fuck are you here? I don't need an audience to watch me suffer!"

"You no know what you say!" Ping raised her hand and pointed her finger in protest, the same way her mother always had. "You no listen, 'cause you want pity. You don't need pity! You need help. Help yourself!"

"Fuck yourself!" Vera screamed.

"Take that back!" Ping warned. "You not know what you say!"

"Look at you! You have everything in the world, including the use of your legs, and you are still jealous over me, and I don't have anything! I've seen the anger in your eyes when your husband looks at me, or when he says something kind. You know your son wishes that his sweet Aunt Vera could be his mother. Then, he wouldn't get slapped and called stupid so much. The one thing I have that you don't is a kind heart, Ping!"

"Your heart not nice. Your heart as black as the vomit all over your face! You never been kind. You try to steal my husband and child, and you turn them against me. I still love you. I still try to help you when you not even help yourself!

Get the fuck up and walk!" Ping rose from her chair and gave Vera a kick to the legs, causing the woman to yelp in pain and grab her chin.

"See that? You felt that!" Ping's eyes grew angrier as she knelt to stare into her sister's face. "If your legs feel, that mean they work. That mean you can walk, you stupid cow! Now get up and walk!"

Vera stared at her sister with all of the hatred towards her that she had developed over the years. Silently, she bore her weight on her arms and etched further towards the low shelf in the corner, the one that held their grandfather's ashes. She repressed the urge to vomit again as she put one hand on the shelf, and then the other. In a matter of minutes, she was pulling herself up. Ping was right, even though her legs wobbled like Bambi's in the start of the old Disney cartoon, she was able to somewhat support her weight, but with more help from her upper body.

"Good," Ping coached. "Now, take two steps, and get your chair!"

'You are a bitch!" Vera took slow, steady movements as she stared at her sister. "If you make it to heaven, mom and Dad will spit in your face. You show no love for family. You disgrace everything they taught us!"

"Walk !" Ping approached her sister with rage. "You not understand! Walk!" She pointed to the window in the corner. "You have to walk. Get going!"

"Fuck you!" Vera let go of the little shelf long enough to grab the teapot. She was too infuriated to realize that she was touching something that contained death and disease. Her fury continued to render her blind as she brought the teapot down upon her sisters head twice, knocking the woman to the floor.

"You silly cow!" Vera stared up at her sister with panic. "You have no idea what you do! No one save you now. You never leave this place either!"

Vera swarmed as Ping slowly faded away before her very eyes. She blinked as she noticed the germ-infested teapot in her hands and the ashes all around her feet and ankles. Once again, she crashed to the floor. Her breathing felt constricted, and her heat thudded. She choked on each breath she struggled to take. Finally, her eyes locked in place.

Later that night

"This is a fucking shame!" Detective Rodriquez ranted as he and his men made their way through Vera's apartment. Her body still lay in the corner, clutching the teapot. "How did the cops who came to take the bodies out of the building downstairs forget that this one here lived just above, and couldn't walk? This is exactly the kind of shit the precinct needs during an election year, when cameras click in our faces each time something goes wrong. Fucking morons!"

"Get this," his assistant began, thumbing through her stack of notes and pictures. "This one on the floor is the sister to the female body we removed from downstairs. The guys in the lab complained to me that wounds appeared on the sister's body, from nowhere, after she had already been brought to the morgue and checked thoroughly this morning."

"Looks like this one here put up quite the fight with something or someone." A rookie cop bent to point out the hair and blood on Vera's hands, and the blood on the teapot her stiff fingers clutched.

The female cop trembled, fighting her need for a cigarette, but remembering the gas leak. "We are going to use the KISS method here, and keep it simple, stupid!" she insisted. "The doors were locked, and there is no way in or out. A gas leak took out her family, who lived downstairs, and here she is, dead, alone, and all of her doors and windows are locked from the inside. This is the result of the same damn gas leak. Less paperwork, less of a headache. Not asking questions, which you know you will never get sufficient answers to, will help you sleep a lot better at night. You will learn to do that a lot more as you grow into this job."

"Right." The young man pushed his short dreadlocks from his face and stood. "Had to be a gas leak." He exited with the other officers, but he knew that he wouldn't be sleeping well any time soon. He would stay awoke many nights wondering whose blood and hair were around the fingers of the beautiful woman that he watched being zipped up in the black body bag. He would recall the look of fear in her open eyes, and always wonder who or what those eyes saw last.

Monster in the closet....Elephant in the room

My ten- year-old brain tried to tell myself that I was dreaming as I opened my eyes. I was shocked into the upright position by a scraping sound in my closet. I fought with every fiber in my being not to turn around, as my fear always made me sleep with my back turned to the closet door, even though I had to make sure that it was closed and locked before I would even lie my head on my pillow.

"Just go away!" I begged through parched lips. "You're not even real." My big sister Kelly-Anne had told me to say that to the shadows and odd sounds that scared me at night. Usually, it would work, and in the morning, Mom would debunk the villain as nothing but a lose pipe whistling under the house, or a stack of coats piled way too high in my room's corner. Something told me that this was neither. I had no toy in my room that would have made the scraping noise in my closet. Also, when I turned my head to face the source of the noise, the cracks of the closet glowed with pale, yellow light.

I told myself that I had to take the chance and swing my body from the bed and hoof it the five feet past the closet, and then another three feet down the hall to mom's room before the creature swung the door open. At least I guess that was the reasoning. All I know next is that I found myself outside of my mother's door, crying hysterically. No sound came from her room. I pushed her door open and ventured inside, preparing to crawl in bed behind her and get scolded for invading her privacy in the morning.

There would be no such luck. Her bed was empty and there was no sound of her stirring in the dark living area. The *thing* had gotten Mom!

Tears caused the journey back to my room to be blurry. I stood outside my door, questioning whether I should even bother to knock on Kelly-Anne or my brother, Bobby's doors. Neither would believe me, let alone be happy that I busted up their precious sleep.

With my head hanged low in defeat, I took two steps into my room. I backed into the hall again as my eyes took in a tall shadow. My heart almost stopped as it left the far corner of my room and approached me.

"Don't scream!" A hand latched onto my mouth as I watched Kelly-Anne's lips form into a duck bill. "SHHH! We have to do this quietly, okay?"

I had no idea what she was talking about, but I was just so pleased to not be alone in the nightmarish situation that I nodded my agreement. She hoisted me up and wrapped a blanket around my shoulders as my legs wrapped around her waist. She ran full speed down stairs, and to the front of the house, where Bobby waited for us by the front door, already dressed in his boots and thick coat.

I had noticed that Kelly-Anne had slid a chair under the closet door of my room, hopefully trapping the vicious monster until we were safely out of the house. Still, all of us stalled at the front door, trembling as we heard it moan and shake the door upstairs.

"Bobby, open the door!" Kelly-Anne's green eyes sparkle with fear as she looked over her shoulder.

'It got Mom!" I announced as we tracked through the muddy yard and down the street to the nearest neighbors' house.

"What is he talking 'bout?" Bobby asked with agitation, his chubby, red face reddening from the run and the cold.

"The thing in the closet!" I croaked. "Mom wasn't in her room when I checked."

"Everybody just be quiet!" Kelly-Anne demanded as we neared the neighbor's house. She instructed Bobby and me to knock on the nieghbors' door and tell them we have an emergency. No less and no more, while she talked to the police on her cellphone.

We were ushered in with welcome and genuine concern, as was the nature of our tightknit community. The mistress of the house prepared beds for bobby and me on the sofa, while Kelly-Anne stayed awake to talk to the adults.

"She was planning to stab Taylor!" I overheard her saying to the oldest daughter, and to my father on the phone later. "Dad, she had this little song: "ilnnnie minnie miney moe…too much children… one must go." She had been humming it for days, but I never caught the words until tonight. I heard her singing it to the top of her voice as she walked up and down the hall. Poor Taylor could have …"

The neighbors' oldest daughter caught a glimpse of me eavesdropping and cleared her throat, pointing out to Kelly-Anne that I was in the doorway.

"Just get here fast Dad. I don't know what to do. Taylor is fine. He doesn't know a thing."

Until I had heard Kelly-Anne on the phone, I had been alright, and I didn't know a thing about the fact that my own mother was a monster, hiding in the closet prepared to do her own child in; and for what? What could I have done that was so bad at only ten years old? I didn't leave my sweaty gym clothes scrolled around the house like Bobby, and I didn't have to get yelled at for taking too long in the shower like Kelly-Anne. Mom used to call me her sweet child. What had I done to change that?

Kelly-Anne's light green eyes glowed from the flashing light of her phone, the only light in the kitchen, where the three oldest women sat up eating cookies and coffee. "Yes sir! I am the one who called. I am her daughter. Well thank God nobody was hurt. Where will you be taking her?" She motioned with her shaking hand for someone to give her a paper and pen.

My guts dropped in my stomach at the idea of Mom being alright. To me that meant that she was free to ty to off me again, any time I left the toilet seat up or got a bad grade on my spelling work, or whatever it was I had done this time.

Whenever I sneaked out of bed to watch horror movies with Bobby, he would tell me that I had to see the movie until the end, to make sure the monster was dead, and then it couldn't haunt my dreams that night. The monster from my closet wasn't dead, and everyone else seemed as if they wanted her to get better and come home to us. Of course they feared nothing. I was the one chosen to go. She handpicked me.

(Thirteen years later)

After spending the next eight years with my father, while Bobby and Kelly-Anne insisted on taking care of mom, I headed to college, where I bombed after two semesters. One good thing came of that wasted time, and that was my introduction to my wife, Heather, who was now pregnant with our fourth child in five years.

I did pretty good for my family, working tiresome hours at her father's car rental service, and also at a local bar, but outside of Heather and my children, I had little friends or family. Bobby only called when he needed help with his gambling debts, and Kelly-Anne was busy with her three kids, who would all be off to college soon themselves. We all lived in different states. Bobby was hiding out in Texas when we had heard from him last, Kelly-Anne had settled into the North Carolina suburbs, and I had moved to Florida to be with my wife's family.

None of us ever talked about the night Mom went crazy, nor did we discuss what may have caused it, though I had a million questions. I wanted to know how those two could just go back and live with her, as if nothing had happened. I wanted to know why they treated me like Judas for wanting to stay with my father. How could they have not thought that staying with Dad was a better idea as well?

"She needs us, Taylor. All of us!" Kelly-Anne had tried to assure me, but I couldn't help but wonder why anyone would try to kill someone that they needed.

Mom had said that there were too many of us, and I was the one chosen to go. That only equaled up to the old saying, last hired is first fired, to me. Kelly-Anne could forget all about me feeling sorry for the woman who had just struck her across the face and called her a trader bitch for putting the chair in front of the door that saved my life. That infamous slap is the last memory I have of my mother while alive. I wish I could say it was the last memory all together

I put off going to Kelly-Anne's place until the last minute, arriving the day before the funeral. As I had told my wife, who was far too pregnant to join me on the trip, I was returning only to take some of the stress away from Kelly-Anne. I had no grief to offer, nor did I have any fund memeries of my mother.

"The prodigal son finally returns!" Kelly-Anne smiled, opening her arms to me as I made my way up the driveway.

I could tell that she had been crying a lot, and sleeping barely at all. Her husband and Bobby sat on the porch, too engaged in the bottle of Tennesse whiskey they were dividing to come say hello to me, which was fine. As I had said, I was here to support Kelly-Anne.

"Your two nephews are dying to see their uncle again. You might think they don't remember you, but you are all they have been talking about. Kyle Junior is the spitting image of you, early twelve now, and Bobby, like his name says, looks just like our brother. I just hope he doesn't take too much after him, if you know what I mean."

"You holding up? Really?" I asked, putting my hand on her shoulder as she turned to summon the boys from inside the house.

"I'm the strong one." Kelly-Anne's blueish green eyes sparkle in the sunlight as she pushed wisps of her delicate, strawberry blonde hair from her sunburned face. "Mom's been gone for only a week, and all I hear from our brother is talk about selling the house. Can you believe that?"

"From Bobby, yes I can. You and me had just better watch that he doesn't gamble it up from under you."

"Somebody say my name?" Bobby finally made his way off the porch and snatched my bags from my hand. He put them on the ground and wrapped his massive arms around me, twirling me around in his drunken celebration. "The whole Brody clan is back together!"

"Yeah." Tears welled in Kelly-Anne's eyes as she added, "For the first time since Dad's funeral. Jesus, what is it going to take to make us be closer? We're running out of people to lose!"

"She'll be fine!" Bobby caught my arm to keep me from following Kelly-Anne as she stormed into the house. "Ma wasn't in no pain or nothing like that. It just was her time to go. I guess Kelly got struck with it harder because she was used to seeing her every day. Kind of like how it was for you when Dad passed."

There is was, the first passive-aggressive stab at me for choosing to live a safe life with our sane father.

"I guess I better go freshen up. It was a really long drive." I gave my brother one more hug and then headed to the porch, where I was glad to find my sister's husband nodding off. Not that Kyle wasn't a pleasant enough guy and all, but he and I had said less than ten words to each other in the eight years he had been with my sister. I wouldn't want him to think that the situation should change that. I was only here for my sister.

I fell asleep in my old bedroom, which was now decorated to suit the taste of Kelly-Anne's six and five year old boys. Seemingly, as soon as I entered slumber, nightmares plagued me. I fought to wake as sweat drenched my body and my heartbeat raced. I had become the ten year old boy, afraid of the noises in the closet and under the bed all over again.

I could feel someone or something straddle my upper body, and I finally built up the strength to bolt up in bed, instinctively flinging the intruder to the ground. As my eyes opened, they settle in on Kyle Junior, who had a look of terror on his face as he peered up from the floor.

"Jesus!" I winced, throwing my legs over the small bed. He scooted back as I reached to soothe him. "I'm sorry."

"Mom said to wake you for dinner." He scrambled up from the floor, looking at me as if I were a maniac as he raced for the door.

Kelly-Anne had prepared quite the spread while Bobby and Kyle continued drinking. Both men sat at the table laughing and cramming their mouths full as they belched the scent of whiskey unto everyone else's plate.

"It's a shame Heather couldn't make it," Kelly-Anne offered, though she couldn't stand my wife, and definitely would have had plenty of snippy comments to offer in the event that Heather had come.

"The doctor didn't think it was a good idea for her to travel this far, plus the kids can't stand to miss the days out of school."

"For someone they barely knew," Kelly-Anne added.

"You said that. I didn't."

"Isn't it sad that mom only got to see your two oldest kids once, at ad's funeral?"

"Jesus Christ!" Bobby spit potatoes halfway across the table as he brought his hand down with a thud. "Are we really going to do this? Kelly-Anne, you weren't the only one who cared about Mama. Stop doing that!"

"I was the only person who cared enough to call her, to take care of her when she was sick, and not try to sell her goddamn house the minute her body turned cold, Bobby!"

Kyle reddened with anger and scooted his chair away from the table. "Come on boys; let's go outside for a while."

"You two always do this!" Kelly-Anne blubbered. "You make me feel like a fool for doing the right thing. I couldn't leave her! Maybe I wanted a good life too."

"I'd say you did alright for yourself." Bobby laughed sarcastically. "You and Kyle have been living here, rent free, for how long now?"

"Fuck you, you son of a bitch! How many bed pans did you change when you came home last time, to borrow even more money from Mom? And you..." Her eyes narrowed on me. "Why are you even here? You made it clear to her how you felt when you were small and went to live with Dad, barely a phone call since!"

"This guilt shit stops right here!" I screamed. "You and Bobby didn't have to stay here and play parents to the parent. I was a scared little boy, whom she tried to kill in his sleep, and I made the right choice. How Dad could even allow you two to not come too was well beyond me."

"Dad was a safer choice?" Kelly-Anne laughed. "Oh, yeah. I forgot; you didn't have titties and ass for him to gawk at and beg you to sit in his lap when he got to drunk. That's why you think of him as a goddamn hero!"

"He wasn't a hero any more than Mom was a monster," Bobby interjected. "We can't keep doing this, not the night before we finally lay her to rest. Let all the craziness and anger die with our parents. We're all we have left now, and I plan on seeing a lot more of both of you, especially on holidays."

"You're right." I stood and put my arm around his shoulder, and we beckoned for Kelly-Anne to join us in a group hug. Instead, she turned and stormed outside with Kyle and the kids.

"She's got Dad's stubborn streak," Bobby laughed. "It was good to see you again, little brother. Now if you excuse me, I am going to take a massive dump and then crash on the sofa"

"You want me to make you some coffee? You smell like one-hundred proof."

"I can sleep it off."

"Sleep sounds good."

Though I was tired from the drive and the family tension, I still felt a weird feeling, telling me to not go upstairs to my childhood room. I ignored it, and spent most of the night tossing and turning, trying to keep my feet from falling off the short mattress and being exposed to the unnatural chill in the air.

After much fighting with myself, I was finally asleep again, and my heart was thudding at the sound of the closet door creeping open. I was watching my younger self lie helpless as some dark creature crept closer and closer. When the monster had finally done its slow motioned dance all the way to the bed I could hear Mom's voice: "Innie minnie miney moe, too many children… one must go." Only, it want the young voice I recalled from when I was a child, it was the sick, hoarse voice that she had spoken to me in at Dad's funeral, the one that let me know she wouldn't be long joining him.

My body trembled in real life as I felt something brush my bangs away from my sweaty face. If ought to open my eyes, and for a split second, I swear I stared right into Mom's menacing, brown eyes. I bolted up in bed, and the figure before me disappeared.

"Get your shit together!" I told myself as a delivered a hard slap to my own face. I f ought my way out of the tiny bed and padded down the hallway, anxious to see if Kyle and Bobby may have been generous enough to leave at least one sip in any of the bottles of whiskey. I had no such luck, and decided to go back to my room after a quick bathroom break.

On the way back, I saw Kyle Jr. and Little Bobby sleep in the fort they had built in the living room. I smiled at how angelic and peaceful they looked. They truly did remind me of Bobby and I when we were kids. They made me miss my kids back home, but I knew it was much too late to call Heather at that time of night.

Again, I poured myself into the tiny bed and forced my eyes shut. Breathing noise seemed to come from the other corner of the room, and I chose to ignore it. I was grown. Nothing that I made up in my own mind would tourment me.

Footsteps came next, and then that aweful chant: "Innie minnie miney moe…too many children… one must go!"

I lay there shivering, realizing that I hadn't had a drink, and that I definitely was not asleep, so I couldn't have been dreaming. Cold air covered me tighter than the knit blanket I pulled over my head, and I shivered, waiting for Mom to reach out and give me the death touch at any moment, but she and the awful song she screeched disappeared after a few seconds. I remained in the position I had curled myself in until I was able to shiver myself to sleep.

When I gained consciousness again, it was daylight, and Kelly-Anne and Kyle were screaming hysterically. I ignored my need to relieve myself and ran into the living room, where she, Kyle and Bobby were huddled over Kyle Junior's lifeless body. The child was blueish gray, and definitely dead, yet Bobby cussed and begged the dispatcher on the phone to get someone to the house ASAP.

Without any shame, I can tell you that piss ran down my legs as I thought back to the image of Mom the night before, and of the song she sang about one child having to go. She had taken my nephew with her the day of her funeral, but of course I would never be able to convince my siblings, let alone my own wife, or my shrink, that I was not having another breakdown if I told them a word of what I had seen or heard. Mom had won, and that was something that I would have to live with in silence, even when I returned home, sitting up long nights, watching over my pregnant wife and my own kids, waiting to hear Mom sing that damn song in my house.

Something tells me that I won't be waiting long.

The end

Sight

Lydia Thompson mopped sweat from her face as she lit her third

cigarette of the morning. Before stashing the packet of cigarettes back

between her large, sweaty cleavage, she peered over her shoulder to make sure the elderly patient she had been assigned to care for was out of listening range before giving her boss her a dose of her no-nonsense attitude. "When the hell is the girl that is supposed to relieve me getting here, Margarete? I've been with this crazy man for over twelve hours, so I hope my check will actually reflect that this time!

"How is he doing? Don't you mean 'what is he doing?' Walking around, taking pictures of people that ain't there, insisting that he don't need me, or nobody else, here, 'cause his daughter takes care of him.

"Well, of course, I know she been dead for nearly a decade! That don't stop *him* from insisting that I leave all the cooking and cleaning up to her. Poor fool won't eat a bite unless I tell him his daughter prepared it. Good thing he's blind as an albino bat!" she jumped at the sound of a car pulling into the driveway, and turned the fan backwards in the living room window, hoping to blow out the smoke from the cigarette, which the company forbade workers to smoke while caring for a patient. "I got to go," she informed the woman on the other end of the phone. "Yeah, I think this is her, a real daffy looking little, white girl. She not going to make it with Mr. Porter. Well, if she is all yawl could find, I guess."

"Hello!" the young, white nurse sang as she gave the door three polite raps. "Mr. Porter!"

"SHHHH!" Lydia held her finger to her mouth as she opened the door. "Girl, take my advice, if that man is finally asleep, don't wake him. He is a handful."

"You must be Lydia. I'm Carodene."

"Delighted." Lydia accepted the girl's handshake. "Listen, there are some things you should know about this patient. First off, he is crabby as hell, and stuck in his ways. Despite having diabetes, cancer, and being blind, he insists on doing everything for himself. You got to find ways to trick him into letting you help him. What he can't do for himself, he insists that you leave for his wife or his daughter, Tara; they both dead, though."

Oh!" Coradene shrunk inside as she processed that information. "Well, then how…"

"Yeah, you got to break a few rules, if you want to keep this job. They not here, so they won't know. What's the harm in letting a crazy, old man call you by his dead wife or daughter's names, long as he eats or takes his meds? That's our secret, which has worked for me for three years. The company can't keep nobody else here for him. I only tell you this, hoping that you got the sense to keep it to yourself, and do what I tell you."

"Of course!"

"Good. He's going to ask for salt, even though the food don't need it, and he ain't supposed to have one grain of it. I put a piece of tape over the holes in the shaker, and since he can't see, I give it a few shakes over his food. The sound is enough to shut him up. HE pisses the bed something terrible, too. Of course, I don't mind much, 'cause my sense of smell is shot to hell. You got to have a strong stomach and the patience of Job. Anyway, you'll figure everything else out on your own. Good luck, girl!"

"Thanks." Coradene shuttered inside, once again, as she watched Lydia disappear out of the door. She looked around the once beautiful house, now adorned with only stacks of ancient magazines and piles of newspaper clippings, which had started to yellow with age. Fine decorations lay grouped, and some shattered, beneath stacks of black and white photographs, the kind taken by a very old photographer's camera.

Being only twenty-three, Coradene had only seen those types of pictures and cameras on television and movies. She could barely recall a time when all pictures were not taken by cellphone. Her eyes widened with excitement, wondering what secrets the piles of old papers and clippings must have held. She had to wrap her arms around herself to keep her hands off of the stacks of old pictures. That did not stop her eyes from landing on what her hands could not: an old jewelry box, Tiffany's perhaps. Broken, but still worth more than the car she had driven in on, or the house she had left to come to work. A box with a woman's silk dress draped over it; definitely from a top designer of long ago, now yellowing like the newspapers and old photos.

The rest was less enchanting to the eye, but drugs to the overactive mind that belonged to Coradene. Broken doll parts, vinyl records, VHS tapes, boxed up trinkets, and obsolete electronics, some so outdated that she could not recognize their intended use, all enticed her as she stood in the center of the makeshift museum. She drew in a deep breath, thinking that less than thirteen months ago, she would have long fled the house with as many of the treasures as her tiny Honda Accord could hold, pawned them for far less than they were worth, and then made another trip back for more, even if it meant she had to slit the old man's throat.

"Tara, I need my coffee!" The rugged voice of the patient caused Coradene to jump away from the box she had just built up the nerve to explore. Her heart beat increased as she recalled Lydia telling her about his strange ways and bad temper.

She hugged her white sweater closer around her thin frame as she turned in circles, taking in more of the sight, and thinking of how to respond to the strong voice, or whether she should respond at all. After all, he didn't call her name. He had never met her. He had asked for Tara, his dead daughter. She had been told that the man was blind and senile, not only by Lydia, but also by the home healthcare company. If she played her cards right, she could continue to collect a check for doing nothing at all, besides rummaging through years and years' worth of boxed up treasures.

No! Who was she fooling? Those thoughts were definitely the last tiny pieces of the old Coradene. She couldn't abandon the old man, let alone steal any of his things, not after what she had promised her grandmother. Coradene had literally been given a second chance at life, and she intended to prove to God that she deserved it.

"Yes sir. Coffee is coming right up!" She balled her fist and stuck them in her pockets as she made her way to the kitchen, the only clutter free place she had laid eyes on. She didn't know whether to be proud of herself for obeying the nurturing side that had led her into home healthcare, or angry that the former heroine junkie in her did not override her instinct to carry away and pawn the many expensive things, which the patient was sure not to notice, being blind and all.

"Who the fuck are you?!"

Coradene's heart thudded at the angry tone of the patient, and also by the sound of him falling out of bed. She drew in a deep breath, and stood still, contemplating whether to run out of the house or go check on whom she was told was a sick, old man, who couldn't tell his feet from his head.

You're wrong, Mark! I'm not a fuck up. She thought as she slowly made her way towards the commotion. *I won't be back to you! I can take care of myself, and I can take care of others. That's why I'm here!*

"Good morning, sir!" she chirped as she stood in the doorway to the bedroom, another room which was free of clutter, and so elegantly decorated that it rivaled the best upscale hotels she had ever been fortunate enough to sell her body in.

"You ain't my Tara!" The elderly man was midway the process of dragging himself up on the bed. Every muscle in his arms protruded, making Coradene think that he looked half as young as she had been told he was.

"No sir. I'm…"

"Some corn-fed, white bitch they done sent me, trying to trick me! They think they going to get all the money I worked hard for just 'cause I'm getting old and I can't see good! Well you take your ass back there and you tell them I don't need you! My daughter takes good care of me and my wife!"

"No sir!" Coradene's voice came out more aggressive than she could have ever expected, being as how she had always been easily intimidated. "I can't go back to the company and tell them anything. I don't work for any company. I'm friends with your daughter, Tara. She told me to watch after you while she can't be here."

"Oh. Bullshit!" Mr. Porter cocked his head to the side and turned to face Coradene, giving her the impression that his eyes had just as much sight as her own. "I'll tell you just like I tell that other thang they send here: you can slave and make a fool out of yourself if you want, but I ain't signing no papers that says you did shit for me, 'cause I didn't ask you to. Take my word; you won't get paid, not out of *my* retirement money. I didn't hire you!"

"Fine." Coradene laughed to herself, thinking that Lydia certainly did not seem like the type that would work and not get paid. She decided that she would ask Lydia's secret on how to do so when she returned to relieve her in the morning. As for now, she was here to help, and Mr. Porter certainly needed her help, even if she had to fight with him to get him to admit it. "So, while you have this white slave, what do you suppose you would have me do first, sir? How does some breakfast sound? I make a pretty mean omelet."

"Omelet? What the hell? No. I never ate nothing like that in my whole life! No! You will fix me what I been eating every morning four forty-six years: fried eggs, not sunny side up, but well done. Don't you dare break my yokes, either! I will have five strips of bacon, black coffee, sugar, no cream, and two toasts, no jam, jelly or butter! You got that?"

"Coming right up, sir." Coradene smiled to herself, as she thought of how Mr. Porter reminded her so much of the grumpy customers that, long ago, frequented the diner she worked in as a teen, the only job she had ever held before getting lost in a world of drugs and abusive relationships. She decided that one grumpy customer was much better than the barrage of oncoming grumps she had contented with as a teen. This job had potential to be a cake walk, as long as she continued to look at things from that perspective.

"Wait. Are you allowed to eat bacon?" Her smile never dropped as she perched herself on the door frame, thinking of how much Mr. Porter reminded her of her own grumpy, old grandfather. "You wouldn't be trying to fool a little, dumb, ole white girl, would you, sir?"

"If it's in my refrigerator, I can eat it, because I bought it!" Mr. Porter scooted himself back on the stack of plush pillows and rolled his dead eyes. "You sure my gal sent you?'

"If not, you still got a full day's work, and you didn't have to pay for it." Coradene blew a kiss at the patient as she exited, happy that he could not see it, and that she didn't risk the chance of her actions being taken as inappropriate conduct. She was even more pleased that she had formed her own bond with Mr. Porter, and that she didn't have to follow any of the suggestions given to her by Lyda. Most of all, the fact that she had caused a tiny smile to come to the old man's face with her words pleased her most of all.

"Three eggs!" Mr. Porter called behind her. "Fry them in the bacon grease!"

"Sure thing, sir!" Coradene's smile increased as she walked to the kitchen, thinking that there was no way in hell she would fry eggs in bacon grease for a diabetic patient, even if she had not become a health nut in the past year of her recovery.

"If it's in your fridge, you're allowed to eat it, huh? Well, ain't it just good news for both of us that Lydia puts everything in your fridge? Checkmate, old man." Coradene tried to stifle a laugh as she glanced over the products in Mr. Porter's refrigerator: sodium free turkey bacon, fat free cheese, olive-oil based butter substitute, fat free mayonnaise, and various packages of ground turkey or chicken instead of the beef, pork and other utter nonsense that she had expected.

"Child, do you really have to do that?!" Mr. Porter chastised from his bedroom as Coradene hummed the song her grandmother had always sang while doing household chores.

"Sorry." Coradene laughed and reminded herself to only sing the lullaby in her head from now on. Though she was just a bit more than pessimistic, she told herself that Mr. Porter's agitation would calm a bit after he had his breakfast and morning coffee.

"And where is my damn breakfast, girl? Did you have to raise the chickens before you could get the eggs? I could have sworn I had a refrigerator full of food. You know what, never mind. You can just go back to the place that sent you, and tell them this ain't work out."

"Gave up on me so soon, sir?" Coradene bit back a laugh as she watched Mr. Porter struggle to get out of the plush bed. "Let me sit your breakfast on this tray, and then I will help you adjust yourself to eat in bed. How does that sound?"

"Like more than I asked you to do!" Again, Mr. Porter rolled his eyes. "Just put it on the tray and roll it up here. I can do some things for myself!"

"Of course you can, sir."

"Who taught you to cook like this?" Mr. Porter smiled as he waved the delightful whiffs of steam from the plate towards his face.

"I had to care for my grandmother when she got sick. I was the oldest girl, actually, the only girl out of six small kids."

"Uh-oh." Mr. Porter frowned as he crammed a fork full of egg in his mouth. "What is it with yawl young folks and not liking salt?"

"Do you need more salt, sir?" Coradene thought back to Lydia's advice as she reached in her pocket to get the clogged salt shaker. She stood still in her tracks, noticing that Mr. Porter was digging something from the side of his mattress. The something turned out to be a Ziploc bag full of salt. She shook her head in disgust as she watched him pinch out more than a finger full and sprinkle it all over his plate.

No wonder his blood pressure had not been improving, despite his strict diet. Lydia had not been the only one with tricks up her sleeve.

"Much better!" The old man's smile returned as he motioned towards a chair in the corner. "Well, at least sit down a spell, since you going to watch me like a hawk."

"That's alright, sir. Just call me when you finish up. I will find other work to occupy myself."

"Don't be silly. Ain't no work to be done around here. Between my wife, my daughter, and that ole other thang they keep sending, this place stays cleaner than ever. You done what I asked you to do. Now you can sit down and rest. Keep an old man company. Tell me about yourself."

"About me, sir? Hmmm. I'm afraid that there isn't much to say."

"Well, you still young. You got lots of time to make stories. You got any youngens?"

"No. Well…one, but she's not mine anymore. I was young, and …"

Mr. Porter's face took on an alarmed expression as he placed his fork down and held his hands up, signaling for Coradene to be silent and still. "You see him?"

Coradene instinctively turned her head from side to side, following the direction the blind man appeared to be looking. "Who, sir?"

"SHHH! That other girl never sees him either, but he is here! Hand me that camera under the chair you sitting in. Hurry!" Mr. Porter whispered his command with urgency.

Coradene promptly obeyed and settled back in her chair. Alarm also swept through her as she watched Mr. Porter turn the camera to and fro, snapping pictures of what appeared to be only empty corners of the room, all the while mumbling about how 'that mother fucker think he slick!'. She had not been told by the company, nor by Lydia, that he had any signs of dementia, only that he forgot people's names and thought that his wife and daughter were still alive, typical symptoms of early senility, nothing that would explain the erratic behavior he was showcasing now.

"Not today, mother fucker!" Mr. Porter carefully placed the camera down beside himself and resumed eating. "That flash scares him away. Now, you were telling me about your baby. How come you think she's not yours anymore?"

"It's uh…complicated." Coradene wiped a tear from her eye as she noted that Mr. Porter certainly was not going through dementia. He had settled right back into their conversation, even reminding her where she had left off speaking.

"I didn't mean to make you sad." The old man reached out his hand, offering the napkin from under his tray of food.

"How did you know I was…" Coradene cocked her head to the side in shock as she slowly rose to accept the napkin. "I wasn't making any sounds."

"I can see shadows. I saw your arm go up to your face, and I knew why, because of what we were talking about. I'm also a human being, with feelings. We don't have to talk about that no more, okay."

"I should find something to do, honestly." Coradene patted the patient's strong hand, offering thanks, and then rose from her chair.

"You can run to the store and pick me up some flashes for this camera. I think this one here is about to blow. Also, get me a few packs of double-A batteries and a few rolls of film." Mr. Porter turned his head towards Coradene, who stared at him as if she had never heard of any of the items he had named. "You writing down any of this, chile?"

"Sorry, sir. I'm not allowed to leave you alone, and the company forbids us to take patients with us. It's an insurance thing. Maybe I could bring you the stuff tomorrow."

"Oh hell! I can't wait 'til tomorrow, girl! He's getting closer and closer! Can't you feel him? Didn't I just tell you that this flash is the only thing that scares him away?!"

"Who is he?" Coradene gripped Mr. Porter's hand again, trying to calm his nerves.

"You wouldn't understand. You're just a baby. It'll be a long time before you have to worry about him."

Coradene's eyes widened as she thought of just how wrong Mr. Porter was about her not being familiar with 'him'. The man obviously was not aware of the three times she had died on the dirty floor of her ex-boyfriend's house, having to be revived with either an adrenaline needle to the heart or defibrillation paddles. He didn't know all the years she had spent at her grandmother's bedside, holding her hand and humming sad lullaby's, noticing each day that *his* stench and the presence of *him* grew stronger in the air.

"Don't worry, sir. I have another way for you to keep him at bay." She rummaged through her purse and retrieved her spare cellphone.

"Before I leave, I will teach you how to use the camera on this, okay? It's way more simple, and just as effective." She took a pic of the empty corner, hoping to showcase the bright flash.

"You ain't too bad; you know that?" Mr. Porter patted Coradene's hand as she placed the phone beside him on the bed. "You might just get me to sign those papers for you after all, but don't tell that other ole thang; you hear me!"

"Yes sir.' Coradene smiled with pride. Mark was definitely wrong. She would not be running back to him. Mr. Porter had just unknowingly made sure of that.

Chapter 2

Coradene lay awake half the night, thinking about Mr. Porter, and praying that God, and her personal angel, her grandmother, would watch out for the old man during the night. Though she tried to tell herself that she was being irrational, and that the old man was imagining things, part of her felt for him, deeply, as if he were in instant danger, and there was nothing she could do to help him. She could only compare that feeling to the time she had been kidnapped from her grandmother's house, where she had gone to kick her pill habit cold turkey, and also to care for the dying woman. Mark, her abusive ex, had held her hostage for two weeks, feeding her drugs, which she eventually took voluntarily, hoping that they would curb her guilt from the thought of her grandmother dying alone, probably calling her name over and over.

"It's just guilt," she told herself as she changed from her sweat-soaked nightgown and splashed water on her face. "Mr. Porter is going to be just fine, and so will you. You just need to get some sleep, and stop scaring yourself, Coradene." She smiled to herself, thinking of how much her latter statement sounded just like her grandmother.

Before returning to bed, she read her grandmother's favorite bible verse, Philippians 4:6-7, and then cranked up the fan to prevent another night sweat. She cuddled with the ragdoll her grandmother had made her when she was a little girl, and she drifted off, listening to the whirling sound of the fan blades.

"You came early today," Lydia appraised. "I got thirty minutes left on the clock, and I need that money, so you can just sit and chill for a while, and I will finish up the last of my work. I'm about to give Mr. Porter a bath before I leave. Poor thing worked up quite the sweat, jumping at sounds, and falling out of bed, trying to take pictures of things that weren't nowhere to be seen. It got so bad a little while ago that I had to hide that dam phone from him."

Coradene's face grew concerned. "How long ago has it been since you last checked on him, Lydia?"

"I just left out the room with him before I came to let you in." Lydia stared at Coradene with questioning eyes. 'What's the matter?"

"Did Mr. Porter ever talk to you about the shadow?"

"He says a lot of crazy mess, but most of the time it ain't to me; it's directed to his dead daughter or his deader wife. I just happen to be there when it's said." Lydia wiped sweat from her brow and shook her head as she stared at Coradene. "You letting him get in your head with that mess already, girl?"

"No. Of course not." Coradene forced a smile and followed Lydia down the hall to Mr. Porter's room.

"I been waiting on you!" Mr. Porter smiled at Coradene, once again giving her the impression that he had perfect vision. "That thang over there done took the phone you gave me. Nearly got me killed! Lucky I had this under the bed." He waved a tiny flashlight as he spoke.

"What the hell, girl?" Lydia stared at Coradene with chastising eyes. "You gave him that phone? You can't give them things, and you can't take anything from them. Didn't you read the rule book? The office will flip out!"

"Sometimes we have to break a few rules to make the job easier!" Coradene retaliated. "That's the first thing you said to me; is it not?"

"So, you think playing into his delusions that some shadow man is coming to take his soul is making this job easier for you or me?"

"Not for us, but for him! It makes him feel better, Lydia. Before you leave, I would appreciate you telling me what you did with my phone." Coradene broke eye contact with Lydia, but made up her mind that she would continue to stand her ground. "I'll be in the living room while you finish up *your* part of the job."

"He's all yours," Lydia said with a hint of hostility. Without making eye contact with Coradene, she headed straight for the door. "Your cellphone is in the nightstand beside his bed."

Coradene promptly sprang from the couch and headed towards the man's bedroom. As she had sat in the living room, replaying her visions and dreams from the previous night, and pairing them with what Lydia had said about Mr. Porter's behavior during the night, she had been overtaken by the urge to make sure that he was okay, even though Lydia had just left. When she reached the end of the hall, she paused outside the patient's door, listening to his deep sobs.

"It's going to be okay, Mr. Porter," she promised walking towards his nightstand. She retrieved the cellphone, and instinctively began to scroll through the many pictures Mr. Porter had taken the night before.

Most were just dark screens, but, as she continued to scroll, the darkness began to take on more and more of a human shape. Her heart stopped in her chest as she looked at the last image, a close up of the shadow's face, or what would have been a face, on a normal being. "Shit!" she wheezed, so frightened that the cellphone dropped from her hand.

"You see him, don't you?" Mr. Porter looked more worried than excited that someone else finally knew that he was not crazy. "When did you pass over? Only someone who been to the other side or is ready to go to the other side can see him. You certainly don't seem like you near ready to meet him, not now. So, when did you cross over?"

"Which time?" Lydia shook her head, deciding that she would not be sharing her dark past with the distressed patient. "That bitch will not be taking your phone again. I'm making sure of that."

"No!" Mr. Porter grabbed her arm as she raised her cellphone to dial the company's number. "You can't do that. If you report her, they will only take it out on you. She been there longer, and she's kin to the owners. If you don't get fired, they will transfer you. I need you here; only you can see him!"

"She could have gotten you killed." Coradene was so frustrated that she could no longer hold back her own tears.

"Shit, you think I ain't never reported that hateful thang? She ain't nothing near as friendly as she pretends to be when you're here to watch her! She stole twenty dollars off my cabinet once, and then had the nerve to make me feel crazy for asking about it. The woman smokes in my house, despite the fact that I'm a cancer patient. Reckon do she think I can't smell 'cause my vision is going? They know about all of that, and she's is still here. Just be quiet, if you want to be here too."

"We'll think of something," Coradene promised. She wiped her eyes and patted Mr. Porter's trembling hand as she promised to return with his breakfast shortly.

After gathering all the ingredients to make his meal, Coradene lamented over the fact that he had not barked his strict menu to her today. Either he had truly grown to trust her, or he was so shaken up by the threat of the shadow that he didn't care, one way or the other, about breakfast.

"Oh great!" she fused, noticing that the pilot light on the oven had gone out. She thanked God that she was familiar with that type of outdated stove, thanks to caring for her thrifty grandmother. She turned on the gas and rummaged around in the drawer until she found a pad of matches. As she bent to light the pilot, Mr. Porter's screams snatched her away from the task. She forgot to cut the gas off as she rushed towards his bedroom.

He lay sprawled out on the floor, only his head moved violently from side to side. His eyes bulged with fear. The camera phone she had given him lay a few feet away on the bed.

"Get away from him!" she screamed, aiming her phone towards Mr. Porter and snapping photo after photo as she walked closer. She finally stopped when the old man was able to sit up and clutch his chest.

"WE got to get out of here!" he warned. "NOW!"

"Okay…okay!" Coradene hurriedly helped Mr. Porter walk over to his wheelchair, and then ran down the hall, pushing the chair so fast that both she and he nearly toppled over.

"He won't stop!" Mr. Porter broke down in tears again once they had reached the safety of the driveway

"You'll be safe tonight, sir!" Coradene promised, wheeling the chair towards her car. She was so caught up in her mission to save the old man that she didn't recognize that her job was being put in jeopardy until the car was wheeling down the highway. Even then, she didn't care. Her only concern was keeping the shadow away from the frightened old man. Insurance risk or not, she was glad to have him in the car with her, safe, instead of waiting alone at the house for God knows what to attack him again.

"My Zorah saved me," Mr. Porter said, staring at Coradene with teary eyes. "She was there, prying that mother fucker off of me. So was my baby girl. You believe me don't you?'

"Of course I do. I wouldn't have taken you away from there if I didn't."

"There was a third lady there too, a pretty white lady with the kindest eyes I ever saw besides my Zorah's. She helped them."

"I'm afraid that was me, sir," Coradene gave a smile, though she was now questioning if Lydia was right. Maybe the old man was crazy, and she was a bundle of nerves from barely sleeping. She began to wonder if she had imagined seeing the face on the camera.

"It wasn't you!" Mr. Porter protested. "Don't you go thinking I'm nuts now! You just said you were on my side!"

"I am." Coradene apologized. "Just don't go telling the people at the hospital this stuff. I bought you here because you were having chest pains. That's all they need to know, okay?"

Mr. Porter sucked his teeth and stared out the window as Coradene wheeled the car into the hospital parking lot.

"I believe you! Honestly." Coradene promised, though she wasn't so sure anymore. "I will sneak this under your pillow before I leave, just in case."

Mr. Porter's eyes brightened as Coradene showed him the cellphone. "You are alright with me."

"Likewise." Coradene reached over and patted his hand. "But no talking about the shadows while we are here. This is the only way I can help. Do you understand?"

"Yeah." Mr. Porter nodded in agreement. "But please, don't forget to leave that phone."

"I wouldn't dare, sir!"

Chapter 3

Coradene's night blurred into a repetitive cycle of the same two nightmares. The first was of her grandmother dying alone, calling her name, no different than any of the times she had dreamed it in the past year. The other dream was of Mr. Porter, being snatched from his bed by the shadow, the nurses and hospital staff, carrying on with their normal business, oblivious to his silent screams of distress as the tormentor dragged him all around the hospital room, shaking his lifeless body like a rag doll. The latter dream bothered her the most, because she still had a chance to help Mr. Porter. She just had to figure out how.

As soon as the hospital would allow visitors, she dragged her sleep deprived body to her car, and then set off towards the hospital, gulping down black coffee, and blasting the radio to keep her from nodding off.

Once she arrived and checked in, a nurse advised her that the hospital usually did not allow any visitors that were not family members, but that she would make an exception for Coradene, only because Mr. Porter had worked himself into frenzy, asking for her all night and morning. She hoped that her presence would calm the troubled man.

"We gave him a mild sedative," the portly nurse explained, ushering Coradene into the room with the sleeping patient.

Coradene's eyes widened in panic. "How long has he been sleep?" She walked over to Mr. Porter and checked his pulse. Only when she saw that he still had one, did her own heartbeat resume.

"He's fine, sugar!" the nurse assured. "Are you okay? You seem a bit frazzled, if you don't mind me saying so. Maybe we should have somebody look at you while you're here."

"I'm fine." Coradene waved the nurse away. "Could you just give me a few minutes with him?"

"Sure. If you need anything, just press that buzzer, okay?"

Coradene rolled her eyes as she noted an essence of judgment in the nurse's phony smile. Sure, she looked like warmed over shit from two nights without sleep, and of course, she was acting like a raging lunatic, but the last thing she or Mr. Porter needed was a sedative.

Before sitting, she adjusted the blanket for Mr. Porter, and then emptied the last few drops of caffeine from her thermos. She didn't know why, but she was suddenly overtaken with urgency to scroll through the photos she had taken of Mr. Porter the day before, just before she had brought him into the hospital. As she clicked on each frame, her need for sleep was quickly replaced by raw adrenaline. Not only could she see the shadow perfectly, but just as Mr. Porter had reported, three female forms fought to free him from the clutches of the dark figure. One of those figures reminded her too much of her grandmother.

"He's been chasing me for years now." Mr. Porter's groggy voice caused Coradene to jump in surprise. He flashed a smile and continued his story. "1994 was the year I first caught that bastard on film. I was a young, healthy man, able to outrun any athlete and out lift any body builder, and then I made the mistake of bringing my camera to the cemetery. We were burying my wife's aunt, and I decided to hang around and snap a few pics afterwards. I caught him on film, and he ain't gave me one day's peace since then." Tears pooled on the old man's cheeks as he spoke. "He took everything from me but my last drop of life, and if it wasn't for my wife, my daughter, and your grandmother, he would have got that yesterday."

Coradene eyes bulged as she stared at the patient. "How did you know that it was my grandmother who helped you?" She rose from her seat and walked over to show Mr. Porter the picture in her phone.

He waved it away and continued talking. "My Zorah came to me last night, just like she did the night that that mother fucker took my daughter. She told me that I was safe now, because your grandmother and my daughter were holding him at my house. He didn't follow me, and he didn't follow her here. He has no idea where I am. For now, I'm as good ass off his radar. But I can't go back to that house, and I won't! He is waiting there, just waiting to pounce on the next person that walks through that door; that's what Zorah told me. I will tell you one thing, that person sure won't be me!"

Coradene stared at the old man with amazement. Even with all of the evidence, and everything that he spoke of lining up perfectly, she wanted so badly to believe that everything was in his mind. Maybe she needed that notion in order to hold on to the last tiny shreds of her own sanity.

"You didn't sleep good, did you?" Mr. Porter smiled as he stared at Coradene. "You have bags under your eyes the size of the iceberg that hit The Titanic, sweetie."

"How did you…"

"The same way I can see that you missed a button on your sweater. I can't explain why, but after what happened to me yesterday, I can see clearly now, not just shadows, but clearly!" He put his finger over his mouth, indicating that he wanted that information to remain a secret.

"Oh no!" Coradene's heart thudded as she processed another dangerous situation in her mind. Mr. Porter was no longer in danger, not as long as his wife, daughter, and her grandmother, were holding the shadow at bay. There was one more person who was in grave danger. "I'll be right back!" she promised, stepping into the hall to make a phone call.

....

"Girl, I can't tell you how good it feels to be able to concentrate on my job without having to run back and forth to see what his crazy self is doing!" Lydia stretched herself out on Mr. Porter's couch as she spoke to the home healthcare manager on the phone. "Yeah, I finally boxed away a few piles of this mess, he keeps scrolled everywhere. I know I'm going to have hell to pay when he gets back, but, it's becoming a risk to both of us."

She reached between her breasts to retrieve her pack of cigarettes. "Oh, he is in love with that little cracker! She come through here one day, and he treating her ass like a long lost member of the family. If I knew that was his thang, I could have talked *like this from day one*," She gave her best impression of Coradene's country accent. "And he would have never known the difference. Blind ass bastard!"

She put down her cigarette lighter as quickly as she had raised it, and left the unlit cigarette dangling from her lip as she stared at her phone, questioning who was attempting to reach her. "Girl, let me call you back. Speak of the devil; here comes little miss trailer park, cutting in on this call right now." Lydia fanned herself as she reciprocated the laughter on the other side of the connection. "Yawl have got to get this bitch straight about the boundaries of the job!" Her eyes glinted as she added, "Never mind. Let me do that for you right now!"

Again, she lowered her cigarette lighter as she cocked her head and awaited Coradene's voice. "Hello?"

"Where are you, Lydia?" Coradene asked with urgency.

"I'm at work, where I'm supposed to be. Is there a reason you're calling and disturbing me?'

'You have to get out of that house, Lydia. I can't explain it to you right now, but you have to get out now! Mr. Porter said…"

"Look, I don't know what kind of stuff you're on now, but this has got to stop! Mr. Porter's paranoia has gone through the roof since you took this job. You've been showing up and barging in, unannounced, during my shift, and you keep entertaining these crazy notions of his, if you're not putting them in his head! I'm going to talk to the agency about this shit."

"Listen, bitch; I'm trying to save your life!"

"Oh see, now, that's where you just fucked up! You need to watch who you disrespect, and you just got the wrong fucking one! Don't think I don't see through your sweet, nurturing routine, saltine! You aren't changing diapers and cleaning up behind old, black people because it gives you joy; bitch, please! Everyone at the agency knows about your problem with drugs, as well as all your relapses, and we're only taking a poll on how long this stint of sobriety will last. I say it ends today, once I get your ass fired, and you realize that you won't be able to even find a job emptying slop jars anywhere else with the name you've made for yourself!"

"You don't know shit about me!" Coradene closed her eyes as tears walked down her face.

"I know you bitch! I know you're trying to befriend that poor, old fool, 'because he ain't got no family or no sense! You just waiting for him to kick the bucket, ain't you, bitch? Maybe by then, you would have fooled him into signing over this house, along with anything worth selling to support your white trash habit! How was that for a guess, *Brittney*? Yeah, that's right. We know your real name. Using your middle name as an alias was a really smart move, though, Saltine. It's over for you!"

"Please. Just listen to me!" Coradene balled her fist in frustration as she listened to Lydia's hysterical laughter. "You have to get out of there, Lydia. For God's sake, why don't you just shut the fuck up and listen?!"

"I ain't got to do shit that the agency didn't tell me to do! I will draw my last breath before I ever take an order form some washed up crack ho!"

Coradene listened to the sparking sound of a cigarette lighter, followed by a few seconds of laughter, and then a big boom, accompanied by a scream. Only at that moment, did she recall that she had forgotten to turn the gas on the stove off before leaving the day before. She dropped her phone in her purse and sadly walked back in to sit with Mr. Porter.

"Is everything okay?" The old man asked, noticing the look of exasperation on Coradene's face. "Don't worry. He's not here. Everything will be fine, as long as you just don't go back to that house."

"Yes sir." Coradene fought to reciprocate the old man's smile, but she knew that everything would not be okay for her. The shadow had claimed Lydia in Mr. Porter's place, but who would it set its sights on next? She had been the only other person to see him, so the answer seemed clear enough. She would spend the remainder of her life, chasing the shadow away with her camera, losing everyone around her, along with her health, and awaiting someone else with the gift of sight to come relieve her of *his* curse, just as she had unknowingly done for Mr. Porter.

Monophobia

"You guys never like anything I share!" Deandria pouted and pushed her glasses back on her nose as she ejected the VHS and carefully put it back in her oversized purse, really a plain, white, cloth shopping bag, which she had painstakingly decorated with horrific drawings of iconic horror scenes and famed serial killers. "I'm starting to think it's because I'm the only one here with boobs and good taste!"

"Boobs, yeah, good taste, not so much." Anderson rose from his seat on the mildewed beanbag and stretched his long, lanky legs before bending to rummage through his own backpack for his special contribution to the Horror Club's secret meeting. He continued to talk as he fished through his surplus of comic books and sketches. "Did you really think we would be amazed by an old *Faces of Death* video? That crap was good for a shutter decades ago, before the web made it possible to see things ten times worse just by signing into your Facebook account." He stood straight, brandishing a VHS cassette of his own. "This, on the other hand, is something that you won't find online. In fact, you won't find this anywhere else, because the powers that be made it go away. The only reason I have this copy is because my grandpa's brother worked for the production company way back in the early eighties."

"It's a fucking porn!" Deandria shook her head with disgust as she snatched the movie and looked at the faded cover. "Are you kidding me?

"Ummm, no, actually, and it's not just any porn. This is the legendary porn in which Misty Walls dies midway a forty-guy gangbang, and they are all so drunk and high that they continue to fuck her for at least two hours before anyone discovers she overdosed."

"Fucking gross!" Carlos rolled his dark eyes and brushed his long, wavy hair from his face. "I'm with Dee on this one, guys. You can see porn at home, on your own computers. I don't want to look at vag and boobs, dead or not"

"See Deandria, you're not the only girl in the club." Anderson gave Carlos a sinister smirk. "Well, what did you bring, *Carla?* Maybe another one of your grandmother's spell books? Why don't we sit in a circle again, and chant words that we can't even pronounce right and wait for nothing to happen again? Sure was a load of fun last time."

"I let you get away with calling me Carla one time, and one time only." Carlos rose from his seat as he spoke. "That was only because we were doing what we were doing, and the idea of me being a girl seemed to freak you out less. Today, I'm going to show your little, cracker ass this Latin machismo!"

"'It's not that serious!" Mark reached out and grabbed Carlos as the boy approached Anderson, ready to punch him in his arrogant face. He flashed Carlos the flirtatious smile that always made the boy calm. "Different things scare different people. Anderson keeps at you with the gay jokes only because his fear that he may be just like you scares him way worse than any movie, dead body, or campfire story ever could."

"What the fuck does that mean?" Anderson literally turned red with anger as he pushed his curly, blonde hair back behind his ears. He crossed over to the other side of the room, knowing that he didn't have a chance in hell of winning a fight against Mark, the boxer from the bad side of town. "Fine! Take his side again, baby him up, and suck his cock. It doesn't matter to me!"

"And what about you?" Deandria's eyes smiled as she noticed that the last member to join the group had arrived late. Unlike the other boys, who all competed for attention, Shane sat quietly in his usual place, as he always had whenever he sneaked in undetected by the other members. While the boys found him to be creep and annoying, Deandria found him fascinating and dreamy.

"Shit, man! Where did you come from?" Carlos grabbed his chest in shock as he followed Deandria's eyes to the boy in the corner.

"I know right!" Mark rolled around on the floor, overtaken with laughter. "Fuck, Shane! This is a horror group, but you aren't allowed to just creep up and scare the shit out of everyone anymore. I'm not trying to die of a heart attack at seventeen!"

Carlos still held his chest as he said, "Announce yourself from now on, dude; we mean that!"

"Sorry." Shane cast his brown, sad eyes to the ground in embarrassment. "It's just that, well…you were all fighting when I came in. I didn't get the chance."

"Don't worry about it." Deandria smiled at Shane. "What did you bring for us?"

"Again?!!!"Anderson scowled with disappointment as Shane gave his usual shrug, signifying that he had nothing to share. "Fuck! You know what? At some point you're going to have to share or not come. You do understand that, right?"

Carlos and Mark rolled their eyes in unison and tried not to look at Shane, whom they had both come to the conclusion was probably homeless, or at the least, extremely poor. To them, the fact that the kid wore the same jeans and white t-shirt, always appeared tired and emaciated, and never had a book, movie, or anything else to share, proved that he was not as up to par, financially, as the rest of the group.

"Asshole!" Carlos gently kicked Anderon's foot and flashed warning eyes.

"It's okay. I'm sure you will come up with something next time, Shane. I sat here, without saying a word, for at least three meetings before I built up the nerve to share anything." Dendria tried to soothe the situation.

"This is like his thirtieth time, not the third!" Anderson protested, despite the harsh looks he caught from his peers.

Deandria stopped walking towards Shane, whom she had planned to give an assuring hug, long enough to turn her attention to Anderson and flip him the bird. When she looked back up, Shane was making his way out of the room.

"Yeah. Definitely next time." Shane smiled and quickly backed out of the small door of the abandoned warehouse.

"You are a fucking douche!" Mark exploded, staring at Anderson with challenging eyes while pulling on his backpack. "Did you really have to do that to the kid?"

"Fuck that! I only pointed out the rules of the club! Don't make me the bad guy. If we all have to share, why doesn't he?"

"Because, we talked about this the last meeting!" Carlos chimed in, taking a moment away from his task of re-applying his thick mascara. "Maybe he doesn't have anything to share. Why does that bug you so badly? The kid sits there, so quiet that we literally don't even know that he is there half the time. He doesn't eat the snacks, and he doesn't smoke our pot. What really bothers you so bad about him? Is it the fact that he may be poor?"

"Bullshit!" Anderson stretched his legs and walked towards Mark and Carlos. "Poor people are some of the best story tellers, have been, since the beginning of time. Many great authors were beggars, telling stories for their supper! Tyler Perry slept in his car for three years, for fucks sake! See? Nobody said his contribution had to be anything materialistic!"

"Just take it easy on him from now on!" Deandria chided. "You don't know how life is for him. This group was formed to bring us misfits together, remember? Carlos has the whole gay thing, and Mark is the only black kid in the whole school. You can't make friends because moving around, and being an army brat your whole life has made you socially retarded, and as for me, well, let's just say the skinny, cheerleading bitches look at me like the town's women did Belle in *Beauty in the Beast*. They will never understand why a girl would rather spend her time reading, or hanging out with you three misfits, when she could be flipping in a short skirt that keeps going over her head, while competing for the affection of some jock, who will be bald and fat in less than decade after graduation."

"That's kind of another thing that fucks with me!" Anderson waved his finger back and forth in the way he did whenever his mind worked faster than his mouth could produce words. "We know everything about each other, but NOTHING about that kid. We just look up one night, and he's following behind us like a damn lost puppy! What the fuck is that?"

"Right!" Mark stepped in front of Anderson to look in his eyes as he made his point. "We were looking for a place to hold these meetings, after the old restaurant got demolished. If that kid hadn't shown us this place, where would be doing this? This place is his contribution, you asshole!"

"I second that!" Carlos held the door open, waiting for his friends to join him "All in favor of counting that as the only contribution Shane has to make, say 'I'".

"I," mark and Deandria agreed.

"Cool. Meeting adjourned. Anderson, blow out the candle in the far right corner, since you are the last person, as usual."

"And you are the first one to race towards the door, just so you won't have to walk ten feet in the dark, you fucking chicken shit!" Anderson shot back. "I won't give that kid shit again, but I'm telling you all, something is sketchy about him, and I can sense it. I bet he isn't even poor. Maybe he is just one of those fucked up Emo kids, and he wears the same shit every day to make him appear dark and troubled. He probably has like sixty pairs of the same jeans and that same shirt."

"Why the fuck would you ever need anyone else to tell you stories when you have an imagination like that?" Mark teased as he filed out behind Carlos and Deandria.

"And another thing!" Anderson started when he joined his friends, "The way he just sits there saying, 'That wasn't scary,' each time somebody shares a story, or whatever, it just makes the hairs on my balls stand on edge. Like…Dude, you contributed nada! Can you at least give props to the ones who did?"

"What else makes you sore about the kid, Anderson?" Mark stopped walking and stared at Anderson. "Does the fact that Deandria has the hots for him have anything to do with you not having one pleasant thing to say about the guy?"

"Oh shit!" Carlos laughed and waved his hands in excitement as he looked from Deandria's embarrassed face to Anderson's face, which was reddening with anger.

"I do not have the hots for him!" Deandria protested, 'and Anderson certainly does not like me in that way! That would be crazy. He's like my brother. That would be like…like incest, right?"

"Exactly!" Anderson's jaws tensed as he brushed past Mark, and then quickly walked past his other two friends. "Assholes!" he screamed behind himself as he felt the first drop of moisture form in the corner of his eyes.

"EWWW!" Deandria whispered as she watched Carlos and Mark gesture that Anderson really did have feelings for her.

"You sure you don't want a ride?" Mark called behind Anderson. When he didn't get a reply, he shook his head and laughed to himself. "Not like he ever offers me any gas money anyway."

"Right. Only gas! It will also be nice to not have to be cold because we have to roll down the windows to survive his monstrous farts!" Carlos added.

"Come on, guys!" Deandria chastised. "Don't you see that you are doing the same thing to Anderson that we just got on him about doing to Shane? Damn, what do you guys say about me when I'm not around?"

"Sure you want to know?" Mark bucked his eyebrows as he gave Deandria a slick smile.

"EWWW! Never mind!" she laughed. "I have seriously got to find some other girls that have advanced beyond Judie Bloom books to induct into this circle of testosterone."

Tears escaped Shane's mysterious eyes as he watched his four friends from the top floor of the abandoned warehouse. His heart sank as the closest things he had to real friends, to real life, vanished into the dark parking lot. How long would he have to await their return?

Time had begun to blur for him nearly a year ago. His entire concept of reality had morphed into that one night, when fate had made him bump into the four kids, the ones who regularly sat in the basement, two floors away from his decaying body, telling macabre tales and gorging themselves with junk food as they watched slasher films.

"That's not scary!" Shane rolled his eyes as he mimicked Anderson' earlier imitation of him.

What would any of those over privileged bastards know about fear? Shane knew fear oh too well, and it certainly was nothing as pleasant as the jump scenes in their cheesy cult classics. Fear was running for his life in the middle of the night to escape the temper of his alcoholic father. Fear was the feeling he had when he forced himself to break the window of the dilapidated building, where the town stored its huge display of ghouls and goblins for the annual Haunted Carnival. Fear was literally jumping as he bumped into every waxed figure, covered in plastic, as he made his way through the pitch dark building. Fear was huddling on the ground, and forcing himself to keep his eyes closed as what he hoped were large rodents, scurried and carried on feet away from his trembling body.

Most of all, fear was waking up from the floor he had slept on, only to find that he had left his physical body behind. Fear was discovering that the thin jacket he had used to plug the hole in the window, hoping to keep out air and snow, had not done its service.

No. those kids knew nothing of real fear. Shane was sure that they would never witness the horrible things he had seen in life, nor would they ever have to spend their deaths hiding from the dark things, the ones that he had watched drag so many other lone spirits to, God knows where. Though he never knew where the spirits were taken, he was certain their voyage was not a pleasant one, based on the screams and fights that they put up whenever one of the dark shadows locked onto them. Shane had witnessed that act happen many nights, right before the eyes of the living, who were usually too high, drunk, or amped up with excitement of chasing their next high, to even take notice that something so violent was unfolding before their eyes.

That was long ago, when he had first become a spirit, and when his longing for human contact outweighed his fear of those things. Since meeting the four living kids, he had decided to play it safe, and to spend his nights in the confides of the moldy building, awaiting the next time his friends would gather. They were all he had left of life.

"A few more months," he lamented, curling behind his own dead body, cradling himself like a lost lover or an oversized stuffed animal. He couldn't be certain of the time of year, especially since he had learned that asking such questions to his friends seemed to arouse their suspicion. Luckily, the surplus of marijuana that they always smoked had helped aid him in going undetected by them this long.

For now, all he could do to comfort himself was to hold on to his rotting body, and to imagine the looks on the collective faces of the lucky kids when the carnival workers finally opened the doors of the warehouse and happened upon his body. Hopefully, he would still be recognizable. The weather had been kind enough to allow him that much so far.

His smile grew into a laugh as he imagined them calling one another in a state of panic, as his picture flashed over the news, and then they would finally realize that they had been hanging with a ghost for months. His laughter stifled in his throat as soon as it came. He wondered if that realization meant that he would never see them again. Maybe he would. They liked the idea of being frightened. Perhaps they would return from time to time, offering stupid gifts to entice him into communication, like the ghost hunters on the television shows. Would they hold hands and light candles in attempts of reaching out to him, or would he remain alone forever? That idea frightened him more than anything else ever had.

Another Sad Love Song

"You know that's not my thing!" Fernando Parker pushed his best friend's hand away from his face as he choked on the smell of Marijuana smoke. He rolled his eyes at his companion, refusing to get sucked in by the 'What do you have to lose?' stare that Kendrid always used on his other peers. "I'm serious!" he repeated much more sternly. "Besides, we are approaching my yard. Do you think I want to explain to my parents why my eyes are red and I smell like Pepe le pew?"

The two girls that walked on either side of Fernando and Kendrid giggled at yet another of his carton references. Though they all were no older than fifteen, at the most, all in the clique had long outgrown cartoons, or anything childlike. Some had done so willingly, and stupidly, while adulthood seemed to be forced on Fernando, who had to play the male of the house every since his father had taken to staying away for weeks or months at a time, and his mother suffered from fits of depression, which kept her from leaving her bed, let alone tending to him or his younger sister.

"He said he didn't want it!" Sarah reached around Kendrid, pretending to hug him from the back as she took the blunt from his lips and gave it three strong pulls. She handed it off to her friend, Maria, who was not liked by Fernando or Kendrick, but was kept around because she made very good eye candy, and dared to wear things that women twice her age would feel overly-exposed in.

"Are yawl bitches ever going to put in ...Or put out?" Kendrid chuckled, though everyone knew he had not been joking, and often spoke those sentiments.

"Maybe we were.'' Maria stepped in front of Kendrid to run her fingers between her mostly exposed breasts. "Maybe we both were. Did you ever think that your fucked up attitude is what keeps us from paying you the time of day?"

"Exactly." Sarah stood beside her friend and tried her best to mimic Maria's sleazy show, but it only caused the guys to see her as desperate, since they had grown up with her since preschool, and knew that she was more comfortable in church than the night clubs that she allowed Maria to drag her to, all in the name of being accepted and mature. "Nobody's ever going to give pussy to a nigguh that acts like a pussy!"

"Okay…okay!" Fernando waved his hands, giving his friends a serious warning to watch their language as he walked further into his huge yard. The house lights were off, but he could see the shadow of his mother, or maybe his sister, curled up in the porch swing. His baby sister, now twelve, had grown to be the spitting image of her mother's face, height, and stature. She even mimicked the woman's quiet mood swings, and had started to act out with silent protests in the absence of their parents.

Fernando pointed to the porch and warned, "Keep it down." He had made it clear to his friends, many times, that he would not tolerate the language that was used when they were alone to be repeated in the presence of his mother, sister, and especially not his father, the latter of which he only watched his words around for fear, not respect.

"I'll catch up with yawl tomorrow." Fernando's hand trembled as he waved his friends away. He was close enough now to realize that the shadow on the porch belonged to his baby sister, Nia, and he could hear her sobs over the sounds of his mother's "depression CD", as it had come to be called by him and Nia.

All through their lives, they had heard their mother cry herself to sleep to one sappy, sad, love song after the other, mostly about women who couldn't find the nerve to leave relationships that were abusive or destructive, all because their hearts wouldn't let them stop loving their man. His mother was fond of Betty Wright, Syleena Johnson, Sparkle, Angie Stone, and specially Mary J. Blige's sad ballads.

At the age of seven, Nia, who took a beautiful voice from her mother, had won the school's talent show by singing "Love should have bought you home," by Toni Braxton, a song that had been a hit years before her birth. Music, particularly, sad music, had also been a permanent staple in the Parker home. Fernando, who was also blessed with the voice of a heartbroken angel, could recall times when he would lock himself in the room with his sister and sing to her as he rocked her and they tried to escape away with the airy voices of whatever troubled diva their mother had left playing on the huge stereo, all the while, listening to his parents cuss, scream, and beat each other into mere lifeless forms, which would glare at him and Nia through swollen eyes, unable to even realize that they were children, smaller people, who existed to do more than carry out commands, such as "Bring your mama an icepack while you get me a beer."

"Perfectly Worthless" by Syleena Johnson began for the second time as Fernando walked over and hugged his trembling sister. "She's been playing that same song for over two hours." Nia bawled. "I can't get in, and she won't answer the phone! So…"

'Fuck!" Fernando pushed his hair away from his face and stared at his sister just long enough to make her think that he was in control, and that she was not alone. "Go over to Mrs. Lewis' house and call 911. Tell them Mama is in a bad way, and that she won't open the door."

Nia nodded her head and gave her best friend one more strong hug before bolting off in the dark night. She was well aware that Fernando was just as afraid as she was, and that he also held the same thought: Even if they were able to save their mother's life this time, how much of her would be recognizable when she returned from the hospital? The prior month's attempt at taking her own life had left the woman nearly catatonic, neglecting everything that she usually took great pride in, her home, her personal upkeep, and even her two beloved children.

Nia and Fernando had noted earlier in the week that they couldn't even recall hearing their mother sing, something which she always did, no matter how happy or sad she was, in over two weeks. The woman had said nothing at all. When they would lie beside her in bed, she would brush their hair backwards, as if rubbing a puppy. She would hug them, and then stare at them with eyes that seemed to focus on something galaxies away, but she would not venture out of the room to put on her usual concerts as she cooked them huge meals, and she would not greet them at the door after school with her impressions of Whitney, Mariah, Celine, and other singers that she could match note for note. They could only guess her feelings by listening to the lyrics of whichever depressing R&B album she played through her closed door.

For the past two weeks, she had been alternating between, "Not gon Cry" by Mary J. Blige, "Hit on me," By Syleena Johnson, and she had played the song that boomed through the cracks of the glass living room door now more than the rest, "Perfectly Worthless," by Syleena Johnson, one of the most underrated of all the sad divas, but a household name to Fernando and Nia while their peers were arguing over who was the best singer between Beyoncé` and Rihanna.

Fernando was on his third attempt at busting through the door with his broadening shoulders when he felt he stronger arms of an adult wrap around him. He looked up to find a family friend and close neighbor, Darryl Lewis, staring down at him with sympathetic eyes.

The man tried to smile, but his face made more of a nervous tick. "It's alright, Jr." He nodded at the worried boy. He turned the boy around and motioned for him to join Nia at the end of the driveway, where she waited with two uniformed officers. A third officer flashed him a smile that nearly mirrored the stiff, fake, 'it's only protocol' smile that he had watched come and go from his neighbors' face just seconds earlier as they passed one another on the porch steps

The last officer drew in a deep breath and peeped over his shoulder to make sure Fernando was a safe enough distance away to not hear the alarm in his words as he talked into his radio. "Yep. Four times in the past six months. Same woman, same problem. This time the kids and the hubby were absent, so there is no telling what this woman did, or how late we are getting here."

He had misjudged the distance between himself and the children, who clung to one another in tears, literally shaking in the night's breeze as they revisited the horror of finding their mother overdosed, or with slit wrists, many times in the past.

"Why don't yawl come to my house?" Darryl put his strong hands on the middle of each child's back and nudged them towards his yard. "I'll get Merva to cook yawl something. This ain't nothing yawl need to see…again."

"No!" Fernando snatched away and walked closer towards his own porch. Nia followed, taking note that her brother was always very respectful to adults, especially Mr. and Mrs. Lewis. If her brother refused to move from the yard, he must have also expected what she felt in her gut, that their mother was *really* gone this time, and that this could be their last time seeing her, save at her funeral. Neither child was willing to pass up such an opportunity, regardless of the emotional trauma that it was sure to bring.

"What the fuck is all of this?!!!"

The children jumped in their skin, as usual, at the sound of their drunken father, who had just driven up and leaned his head out of his SUV window. 'What that crazy bitch done did now?" he slurred staring at Darryl for an explanation.

Two officers and two paramedics had reduced the wood and glass door to a pile of glass and rusted hinges by the time Fernando senior had staggered on his porch, and demanded to know what the fuck they thought they were doing to his house.

The men continued their main priority as they spoke to Fernando Senior over their shoulders and begged him to give them room to work.

Once they were inside the house, they were met with a second obstacle, a locked bathroom door, which took them a lot less time to break down. After that, they were bombarded with the scent of lavender body wash, and the sight of Paris Parker, slumped over in the bloody bubble-bath that ran onto the floor, her arm leaked blood from a wound that ran from her wrist to her inner elbow. Had her blood and the overflow from the tub not dowsed the many candles at the skirt of the tub, they would have also had to worry about a fire.

Though neither Nia nor Fernando had ever heard their father sing a day in his life, the horrific note that he hit upon seeing his dead wife, seemed to rival Minnie Riperton and Mariah Carey in pitch. It caused the kids to fight for their freedom from the officers and Darryl, who held them back. Fernando escaped just in time to make it to the front door, but his way was blocked by his father, who stared at him with moist eyes, and a face that had been decorated by vomit.

"Take my baby girl to your house!" Fernando Senior begged his neighbor. "She damn sure don't need to see what this fool done!"

Fernando went as limp as his sister had at those words, making it easier for his father to throw him over his shoulder and carry him towards safety, mimicking the what Daryl had done with Nia moments earlier.

Once inside, the kids looked past, or maybe even through, their Godmother, Merva Lewis until Daryl had pried the always overly attentive woman away and begged her to give the children breathing room. Then, they clung to one another in silence, Fernando smoothing Nia's hair down over and over again in the same lifeless and purposeless way that their mother had done them in the weeks prior to her suicide. Nia repeated the action on Merva's pet poodle, Scotch. She thought to herself that scotch must have sensed their sadness, because he was not usually the type of dog that liked to be held or stroked, despite his small size.

"I'm so sorry," Darryl said to Fernando senior, who paced the floor, running his hands through his receding, curls.

"Wasn't nothing you could do." Fernando stopped pacing and gave Daryl a brotherly hug. "I don't know what I would do without you and Merva." He drew in a deep breath and tossed a stack of twenty dollar bills on the counter before turning to leave. "I'm coming back to get them." He used his head to motion towards his children, but couldn't bring himself to look over at them. "But until I can, you and Merva do right by them, please. I know I ain't got to worry about that, but…"

"You never do, and you know that!" Darryl tried to force the stack of wet money back into Fernando's hand.

"I'll be back!" Fernando choked back tears and threw back the shot of Hennessy that had been poured for him by Merva nearly thirty minutes earlier. "Keep that. They eat like horses." He flashed the latest fake smile of the night before pushing Darryl away and saying, "Sheeva is out in the car. She got to be all to pieces. She saw them take that fool out of there like that. She needs me tonight. I know you and Merva got my kids. Thanks."

Even when Nia had broken her silence and began to scream and cuss, Fernando senior did not allow his daughter's cries to let him turn around. He already knew that they came more from anger than pain, the same anger her mother had passed onto her at the mention of his new girlfriend's name. His son felt the same, but like his father, Fernando Jr. was not one to articulate his feelings often.

Chapter 2

Four days passed without Fernando Senior popping in to check on his kids, or giving them a call. Nia passed those days curled in a ball on her Godparents' sofa, cuddling Scotch. Her brother continued his routine of school and afterschool sports, hoping to get some relief from the thick air of silence and the sad sniffles that often cut through the silence, just when it had started to become peaceful. At night, he would curl up at the foot of the large couch with Nia, and they would hum themselves to sleep to the rhythm of one of their mother's depressing songs.

Saturday morning, both kids lay awake, but too sad and afraid of disturbing their elderly godparents to cut on the television or to stir too much. Merva and Darryl, with their failing health, had poured more energy into the children in half a week than either of their real parents had found strength or time to do in the past year. Even though they both missed their mother, and their own home, they couldn't help but find comfort and peace in the normalcy of their neighbor's home. Each had even been assigned a private room, but chose to camp out on the couch to be together most nights.

Fernando winced as he heard the front door open. Always protective of his environment, and especially of Nia, he bolted up on the couch, throwing the blanket to the floor. His sleepy eyes darted towards the door and stared at his father in hatred.

"Yawl good?" Fernando senior asked, shifting in embarrassment as he looked into his son's questioning eyes. He didn't have to hear those questions to feel like half the man he thought his son ever saw him as.

"Merva and Darryl made sure we were okay!" Fernando rolled his eyes, trying hard to keep the words, "Unlike your ass," unspoken.

"I knew I made the right choice. Listen, I need you to come with me to the house. We the men and we got to look out for your little sister. We can't let her see the way that fool left the place; she don't ever need to see that. Me and Sheeva went there yesterday, and she done scrubbed up most of it, but me and you got to replace the carpet and do some other things. Get dressed! I need you to be a man; you hear me?!"

"When you get a chance, you and I need to sit down, with the kids, and start working on the obituary," Merva quietly spoke from the cracked bedroom door. "I called the funeral home, and made some calls to some of her distant family, but I didn't want to overstep my boundaries."

"No such thing!" Fernando Senior waved the woman's words away. "You just as much family as anybody else, Merva. I'm sure you did right. Thanks for holding my kids down, like always." After kissing Nia on the forehead, he pushed his son out the door and followed.

Merva walked over and locked the door before adjusting the blanket over Nia. She turned to address her half-sleep husband. "That was Fernando. He *finally* made it here to check on his motherless babies."

"SHHHH!" Darryl begged as he motioned to the sleeping child on the couch

"I'm sorry, but I hate that man now, and you know I can find something good to say about Satan. What that motherfucker put that woman through, and how he been treating his children since they lost her, it ain't right, Darryl. I love these kids, and I will continue to do for them, but that man is not our friend anymore!"

Nia pushed the blanket from her face and shot up on the couch. "I agree, and he damn sure ain't our father anymore! My mama is gone because he chose a fat stripper over her, somebody who ain't good at doing nothing but making their ass cheeks clap! She ain't as pretty as Mama, and she damn sure ain't got mama's looks, good heart, talent, or anything on Mama! What was he thinking?!"

Merva bent and waved her finger before the crying girl's face. "Any other time, I would smack that grown mouth of yours and tell you to stay in a child's place, but this is the place he put his children, and I know it isn't easy. I also agree with every word you just said."

"Don't Merva!" Darryl spun his wife around and seized her by the shoulders. "It ain't right to turn no child against their parents, no matter what." He turned his gaze towards Nia. "God won't bless you if you go on talking and thinking like that about your own daddy; you hear?!"

Nia bit down on her tongue and nodded out of respect for the older man. Once he had walked away she motioned for Merva to join her on the couch. "All I know is that he better not be planning to bring that bitch to Mama's funeral. We don't want her there, with her big tits hitting everyone in the face, and with those long, red, hooker fingernails and clear high heel shoes. Mama might jump out the coffin and swing on that bitch! Excuse my words."

"Only this once!" Merva laughed. "And I will sit down with your father and facilitate a talk. I never met the girl, and I have nothing personal against her, even though you may have a right to, but it just wouldn't be Godly for her to be there."

"Thank you!" Nia hugged her godmother tight and listened to the song Merva hummed as she stroked her hair, not a sad R&B song, as her mother always sang, but a cheerful Gospel hymn.

Chapter 3

"Did you ever love her?" Fernando Junior stopped his task of cutting the bloody carpet from the hallway floor long enough to wipe his eyes and stare at his father. "I've been alive for fifteen years, and I have never heard you say you loved her. She said it to you all the time, and about you, even when you were not around to hear, but I never heard you say you loved my mama!"

"I did the right thing by her and by yawl. Sometimes, love ain't got shit to do with nothing. I was nineteen years old, a college sophomore when your mom trapped me. I was thinking about what team was going to draft me for the NFL, and what I was going to do with my life after I finished college, but that never happened. She got pregnant with you, and we both dropped out, stood in front of a preacher, and …" The drunken man slumped further in his chair and took another drink from his flask. "Ain't no need to talk about the pass, is it?"

"Mama had dreams and goals too, Daddy! She was touring with famous groups, and solo singers, on her time off from college. Have you heard any of the demos she recorded before she got pregnant and settled down with you? They're great, Dad! Mama could have been somebody, with kids and a husband, or not. Mama had something special, Daddy! I think the only reason she stopped trying is because you didn't want her to! She never said that; I figured that much out for myself. Nobody else's mother that I know can match Patti Labelle or Keke Wyatt note for note, Dad." He wiped his eyes again and threw the last wad of carpet in the wheel barrel. His eyes fixed on his father as he wiped sweat from his brow with his t-shirt. He waved his hand, shooing away the bad vibes that is father's eyes sent before exiting the house and walking back to check on his sister.

"You did have talent, you goddamn fool!" Fernando Senior screamed aloud as he sent the empty flask crashing into the wall in rage. He buried his head in his hands as he released the tears he had hidden from Sheeva and his children for nearly a week. He hoped to get them all out before the funeral, which would take place the next day. He had already planned to sit through the ceremony stone-faced and tearless, just the way his kids had come to know and respect him throughout life. "Why the fuck did you have to do some dumb shit like this for, you fool?!!

When Fernando's self-pity had lulled him asleep, his heart skipped at the sound of the radio coming on by itself. Louder than ever, "Never Gonna Let You Go" by BlackStreet blared through the house, instantly filling his mind with the many times he had danced to that song with his deceased wife, and how she would laugh at his hoarse, tone-deaf way of trying to serenade her. Little did she know he envied her, and wanted to be a part of whatever made her special to him and everyone else. He had laughed along, and kept his hurt a secret for years. Only now, with no children or anybody else present, could he allow himself to wallow in his hurt, and accept the fact that he never felt good enough for Paris Parker, the only woman he would ever love.

Though Paris had never stepped out on him in their sixteen year relationship, Fernando was always looking for something new, young, and pretty to fall back on, usually someone with much less going for themselves than he had to offer. He had long subscribed to his notions that someone as beautiful, talented, and brilliant as Paris was sure to wake up one day, and see him for the worthless fuckup that his father always told him he was. That is why he constantly flaunted other women in her face, as a warning, a bluff that he could do better, and did not have to live with her judgment, though Paris never gave him a reason to believe that she was truly unhappy with anything about him besides that very infidelity.

"What the fuck you think we going to do without you?!" he blurted as he snatched the radio's plug from the wall and stormed out the door. "You ain't the fool, Paris!" he turned to apologize just when he got to the front door. "I'm the fool! I was always the goddamn fool!" He fell to the floor just in front of the door, stretching out his trembling legs as he cried again.

The house was flooded again by the sounds of Adina Howard and Michael Speaks' remake of Rene and Angela's classic song, "You don't have to cry," the version Paris had always favored over the original Rene and Angela recording. Calm washed over Fernando, even causing him to chuckle. The euphoric feeling lasted for the duration of the song, but when it was over, he realized that he had unplugged the radio before the song began to play. His heart sped, but the feeling of joy remained. With a smile, he pulled himself up by the door handle and set out to talk to his children.

Chapter 4

True to Merva's word, she made sure that Fernando did not allow his young girlfriend to attend Paris' funeral. She had even convinced Fernando to spend more time with his children, and after a few weeks, the family unit slowly seemed to repair itself. Though Fernando never talked much about Sheeva, it became evident that he was happy to have time away from the demanding youngster, time to lavish on his own growing kids. Fernando Jr. And Nia had even began to feel more comfortable sleeping in their own home, and had returned to the great students they had always been in school.

All of that changed a month later, the day that Fernando Senior decided that he owed it to himself to no longer have to split time between his children and his new fiancé. He paid every bill in the house, and if his kids couldn't get along with the new woman that he moved in, then they would have to make other arrangements. He decided that he had gone through too much to not focus on himself again.

Nia spoke to her father as she came into the house and put her backpack down, as was usual, she ignored Sheeva's smile and wave, expecting to wait the usual hour or two, until the woman had left, to come out of the seclusion of her bedroom. Just as she had turned the corner to head upstairs, she ran back into the living room. Her nostrils twitched with anger as her doe-like eyes scanned the rearranged living room.

"What the fuck did you do?!" her eyes narrowed in on Sheeva as she pointed to the wall behind the couch. "Where are my mother's album covers?"

Fernando hopped up from the couch and stepped before his daughter. "Whoa! Whoa! First of all, she is grown and you don't talk to her like that! Apologize, now!"

"I don't owe her an apology!" Nia sidestepped her father and stared at Sheeva again. "What did you do with my mother's collogue of classic album covers?!"

Sheeva pointed towards the storage closet, where she had carelessly heaped Paris's beloved records into a large, brown box. "I ain't hurt nothing! I just get tired of seeing those old things hanging around here. It gives the place a nine-teen eighties night club feel. No disrespect to your mother, but this is a house, not a club!"

"Then what the fuck are you doing here? We have no poll or crumpled dollars!" Nia pushed pass her father a he stared at her threateningly. "Never mind," she decided before trying to get him to understand her anger. She turned her attention back towards Sheeva. "Some of these albums are worth more than you make at *your club* in a week! Be careful what you touch around here. Everything here, besides my father, still belongs to my mother!"

"I can't believe you let that little girl get all up in my face like that, Fernando!" Sheeva panted. "This ain't going to work out. I ain't here to be nobody's mama, or punching bag!" her short skirt rose in the back as she leaned over the couch to snatch down the abstract mural she had hanged earlier.

"Don't be like that!" Fernando wrapped his arms around the young woman's waist and kissed her cheek. "They just lost their mom, baby. Maybe it's a little early to start rearranging things. Maybe give them a little time to know you better before you replace their mother's stuff. Okay?"

Sheeva spun around with her hands on her hips. "Maybe I shouldn't have scrubbed up that bitch's blood either, huh? Then everything really would be just like that psycho left it!"

Fernando's eyes narrowed with rage as he struck Sheeva for the first time, slapping her so hard that she fell backwards on the couch. He stared at the young girl with pity, but decided that he owed her no apology. He drew in a deep breath and stormed out of the door. He didn't care whether she would still be there when he returned.

Sheeva was busy checking her face in the collage of mirrors she had placed on the opposite wall when the radio startled her. "He's mine" by the 1990's girl group, Mokensteph, caused her to whirl around in fear. She laughed at the irony as she walked over and pushed the power button. The noise fizzled out, and she breathed in a sigh of relief.

She curled up on the couch, preparing to call her sister and tell her what an asshole Fernando had been for not taking up for her, but her cellphone, which she had just removed from the charger, had a dead battery. She smacked her lips in annoyance, and whirled her head around to check the thermostat. The temperature in the room seemed to drop rapidly. She lay on the couch, trying to convince herself that he only menacing thing she had to worry about was the twelve year old little girl upstairs, but that thought didn't stop the hairs from standing on her arms, or stop her skin from producing small goose pimples. The blanket that she pulled from the back of the couch and wrapped around her was more for protection from the uncomfortable presence than the cold. She wrapped her head and shoulders in the blanket and lay still, even when the radio turned on again, this time blasting,

"Woman to woman" by Shirley Brown. She deicide that either Nia was upstairs playing some cruel joke, via remote control, or the girl's late mother shared the daughter's sentiments about her presence in her home. Either way, she would not move to investigate until Fernando Senior returned. She would even settle for the company of Fernando Jr, who hated her, every bit as much as his sister, but kept his hostility limited to ignoring her.

Chapter 5

"I know it sounds strange!" Fernando sighed as he looked at the faces of his friends. "I'm telling you, it's like she sends us messages through the fucking stereo!"

Kendrid sipped from his water bottle, now filled with gin and juice, and passed it to Maria. He didn't have the heart to tell his friend that his story of a haunted radio seemed a desperate reach for attention. He decided not to speak at all.

"You believe me, right?" Fernando stared at Sarah, whom he had known before any of his other friends. "You know I'm not lying, or being crazy, right?"

"I believe every word you said." Sarah waved the bottle away and walked over to sit closer to Fernando. "I also believe that there is an explanation for all of it. Of course, you miss your mother. When people leave us, we look for answers and messages in everything. Your mom loved music more than anyone I know. Naturally, you would think that a short circuit in your radio is her way of sending you out some weird communication."

"Or maybe it really *is* her way of communicating with us!" Fernando stood and stared at his friends, challenging them to try harder to disprove his suspicion. "Everybody in the house has had the radio come on at some time or another, and play a song that was meant *just* for *them*. For my dad, it was this old song that he and my mama used to dance to in high school! For Nia, it was "Always be my baby" by Mariah Carey (the song my mama used to sing to her when she rocked her to sleep as a baby!), and for me, it was "You'll never stand alone" by Whitney Houston. My mother used to sing that to me to cheer me up when I had a bad day!" He halted at the door, deciding not to tell them the subliminal threats that Sheeva had been receiving through the radio.

"Hold up!" Maria giggled in her usual manner, which suggested that she would reveal some insight that the others were too immature to grasp without her help. She stood to her feet and toyed with the buttons on her phone. "This happened to you yesterday morning? HMM… I think I found your answer as to why you awoke to a Whitney Houston song." She laughed as she extended her phone, showing that the previous day had been Whitney's birthday. "She was only the most popular singer in the world! Of course, the radio stations were playing her music on the morning of her birthday. Duh!"

"I guess so." Fernando left through the side door of Kendrid's attic and headed down the street to his own house, wondering what song his mother would play for them next. His friends could joke, or try to find scientific reasoning, all they wanted, but they couldn't debunk the feel of his mother's presence, or the smell of her perfume, each of which intensified whenever she played the members of her family a song.

It seemed as if Fernando could sense the hostility that exuded throughout the house before he even stepped into the yard. Chaotic screams escaped the cracks of the beautiful brick foundation as he slowly pressed forward. Those screams were highlighted by the blaring sound of a radio loudly playing Aaliyah's, "We need a resolution."

"She wants to get rid of mom's stereo!" Nia explained as soon as her eyes locked on her brother.

"You can't let her do that!" Fernando Jr. instantly pleaded with his father. "You know how important this stereo is to her! Dad, you bought this for her when I was like six years old! She sang karaoke on the microphone for us every day since." He waved his hand over the stereo in protest. "This *is* Mom, Dad! If you get rid of this, it will be like you killed her all over again."

"I think you need to watch what you imply!" Fernando senior stepped before his son in a threatening manner. "What do you mean it will be like I killed her *again*? Do you think I killed her the first time?"

"Of course, not!" Fernando Jr. turned his attention towards his sister who fought with all of her might to keep Sheeva from pushing the large system towards the front door. "Knock it off!" he warned, gently nudging Sheeva's hands away from the machine. "Majority rules, and we say it stays!"

"Oh, yeah?" Sheeva pushed her breast up in her tight shirt and turned to face Fernando Senior. "Majority rules? So far it's two kids against an adult. You decide. Do you want to keep listening to a ghost, or do you want to have a real, flesh and blood woman?"

Fernando Senior ran his hands through his hair and scanned each face in the room. He crossed over to his favorite chair and sat silent for a few seconds. Finally, he pointed to the stereo. "It means too much to them, Sheeva. Come on, it's just a damn stereo! If it comes on by itself, and it spooks you out, turn it back off. That's all there is to it. Like you said, you are a flesh and blood woman!"

"I guess that settles that!" Sheeva cussed in Spanish as she waltzed down the hall. "The dead woman gets the last say in everything!" she fumed before slamming the bedroom door.

"You handled that well," Fernando Senior said to his son. "Your timing was perfect. I felt like Sheeva and your sister was playing tug of war with me instead of that stupid radio!"

"It's not stupid, Daddy!" Nia challenged. "It's *Mom,* and you know that by now, no matter how much you have to pretend in front of Strip Club Barbie, you know that Mama talks to us through that stereo!"

"It's still here. That's all that matters." Fernando Jr. walked over and literally gave the stereo a kiss. "And it's never going anywhere." He turned and stared at his father with challenge in his eyes. "Right, Dad?"

Fernando Senior was about to check his son's arrogance, but the stereo beat him to it, much in Paris' fashion, it began to play Syleena Johnson's "Guess What". All faces wore the same expression as they listened to the songstress belt out,

"You want to wear the pants,

You got to be a man.

Hanging out with your friends;

You better watch what time you come in.

Don't wanna pay the bills?

I know somebody who will."

Fernando Senior smiled at his kids as they all thought back to how Paris would sing that song to keep her son and husband in check. "Yeah. She's here to stay." He held out his arms, beckoning his kids to hug him, something he hadn't done in quite a long while. "She ain't going nowhere!"

Chapter 6

With some nudging from her brother and father, Nia began to make more effort of accepting Sheeva. Fernando Senior had made it clear that only he was allowed to scold or discipline his children, which made the transition into peace a little easier. The fact that Sheeva was almost as good at cooking as their mother helped a lot in making the children warm up to her. Paris had spoiled the three so much that none could produce anything but fried bologna and boiled eggs on the stove.

"Something smells good!" Nia appraised as she walked into the house and threw her book bag on the couch. Her face brightened as she noticed that Darryl and Merva were on the couch, nodding their heads to the 1990's slow jams that echoed through the living room.

"Yeah. Your father invited us here," Darryl nodded. "Said he had a surprise for us all."

Merva rolled her eyes, still upset at the prospect of Fernando replacing her good friend with the young woman, who sang off key in the kitchen. "I hope it's not what I think it is!"

Nia shrugged. "Well, if she's going to live here, and do everything that a wife does, she may as well *be* his wife. Me and Fernando are cool on that. We don't hate her anymore. We've called a truce."

"That's mighty big of you, Little Lady!" Darryl smiled his approval.

"She's not that bad. She'll NEVER be our mother, but she has her moments." Nia purposely elevated her voice to make sure Sheeva had heard her in the kitchen.

"What am I walking in on?" Fernando Jr. asked, walking over to hug godparents. He chuckled as he turned to face Nia. "I thought we agreed to give her a chance."

"Ain't nobody giving her a hard time!" Nia said defensively. "She is okay, as long as she realizes that she is here for Daddy, not us."

Sheeva cleared her throat as she stood in the opening of the kitchen. "Speaking of your father, could one of you give him a call. If he answers for you, remind him that he has company waiting on some big announcement that he gathered us all here for."

I think we all know what that announcement is going to be!" Nia rolled her eyes.

"Well, he's not answering my calls or texts!" Sheeva pouted. ''You would think that he could put his other chicks on the back burner one day, especially since this engagement shit was his idea. I'm supposed to be getting surprised with it all."

A loud popping noise echoed through the room, causing everyone, especially Sheeva, who was closest to the radio, from which the noise came, to jump in fright. Instantly, the radio flashed its lights and "I'm his only woman" by Jennifer Hudson and Fantasia began to play.

"Scared the living daylights out of me!" Merva clutched her chest and smiled as she looked around to see if anyone else shared her feelings.

"It does that." Fernando Jr. waved his hand, signaling for the older neighbors not to be concerned.

Darryl rose from his chair and walked towards the large machine. "Must got a short in the wires. Maybe I should look at it."

"No!" Nia stepped before him in protest, remembering that the wire had been unplugged from the wall for some time, and not wanting Darryl to discover the truth. "Dad wouldn't like that. This is all we have left of Mom. He doesn't even like for *us* to touch it."

"All you have left of your mother?" Sheeva gasped in disgust. "Well, if you want something else to remember her by, why don't you come take your pick from the entire wardrobe of hers that Fernando won't let me move out of the closet? Yeah. All of my designer shit is still in boxes. Meanwhile, her perfume and cosmetics are taking up the entire shelf, like it's her personal store!"

"Darryl, she said no, Honey!" Merva nudged, trying to change the tone of the conversation. "If you want to tinker with something, start with the dishwasher at our house, which you promised to fix three months ago!"

"Everything here is *hers*!" Sheeva nervously lit a cigarette as she paced the small floor that connected the living room to the kitchen. "I swear, sometimes, I feel like she is still here, and she is watching me, just waiting for a chance to attack. I know it sounds crazy to you, but…I do. I wish I could talk to her. I would tell her it's not my fault. I didn't know about her."

Fernando and Nia stared at the radio as the song ended, both wondering what message their mother would send next. They let out a collective sigh of relief when the light flickered and the radio turned off.

Chapter 7

"Well, I wish you two all the best!" Darryl gave his honest smile as headed to the door, followed by Merva, who nodded and tried to hide her contempt for the newly engaged couple.

"Don't be strangers." Sheeva stepped to the door, trying her best to sound welcoming and friendly, even though she already knew that Darryl and Merva were more of a fixed staple in the house than was she. "I sit here by myself most of the days, while Fernando works and the kids are at school. Maybe you two can come over and hang out." She sighed a deep breath as Merva's smile became even more see-through. She felt in her heart that winning the couple over was impossible, but she couldn't stand the thought of being home alone. Even worse was the thought of actually not being alone when she was supposed to be.

"Anytime you need us, you just walk over to the house with the blue trim and give the bell a ring." Darryl tipped his hat and escorted his wife towards their yard.

'I'm off to bed." Fernando Junior stood and stretched his legs. He had been doing the gentlemanly thing and letting Merva have the only seat in the house that was tall enough to suit his basketball player's physique due to her bad knees. "Dinner was lovely, Sheeva. Thank you." he crossed over and gave his future stepmother a hug. "I'm happy for you, Dad." He gave his father a hug too.

Just as Fernando Jr. Turned to head to his room, hi sister burst in from the kitchen. She was so angry that she could hardly speak because of her elevated breathing. She held a trash bag in her hands, and stormed towards Sheeva with a menacing glare in her eyes.

"What the hell did you do?" She poured the contents of the bag out a Sheeva's feet, revealing two halve of what used to be a glass casserole dish. 'Who told you that you could touch this?"

"Fernando Senior shook his head, realizing that Nia's anger spouted from the fact that the dish had been one of Paris' prized possessions, given to her by Fernando Senior's mother as a wedding present. Each of his five sisters had one matching piece from the expensive set of heirlooms that had been handed down to her from her grandmother. Paris had been the only one of her son's wives to receive a piece from the set

"It just popped," Sheeva apologized. I took it out of the oven, and when I sat it on the counter, it popped."

"You shouldn't have touched it!" Tears poured down Nia's face as she stared at her father, who had stepped between her and his fiancé. "As of right now, the peace truce is over!"

"Don't go after her!" Sheeva begged, catching Fernando Senior's arm as he attempted to chase after the child that had stormed off to her room. "Don't you get what they are doing?"

"Who is they?" Fernando Jr. asked. "She said what she said to you because you trashed our mother's dish, a dish that was supposed to be handed down to Nia when she got married. I won't front. I'm kind of pissed too, but I know mistakes happen. I don't have anything bad to say to you."

"Look, they sell these for twenty dollars all day at Macy's. I can buy her another one!"

"No. You can't. It won't be the one that Grandma saved for fifty years before giving it to my mother." Fernando Jr. shook his head in disgust. "You picked a real good one this time, Dad." He patted his father on the shoulder with an heir of sarcasm before sprinting off to his room.

"Don't!' Sheeva chided, covering Fernando Senior's face with her finger. "We will talk about the stupid dish tomorrow. Tonight is our night. Between work, those other stupid bitches you fuck, and this thing with your dead wife, I hardly get to see you anymore. When I do, we spend so much time arguing over kids that are nearly my age, that all we do is go to sleep mad. Not tonight. This was our engagement dinner, and we had to share it with your kids and your friends already. The rest of the night is yours and mine."

"Understood." Fernando Senior smiled as he took Sheeva's hand and lead her to the bedroom.

"You wait here!" he was instructed as Sheeva pushed him down on the large bed and walked into the bathroom.

He was almost drifting off to sleep, having been tired from a hard day of work, and the added stress of dealing with the tension between his fiancé and kids. He fought the urge to close his sleepy eyes in order to avoid another altercation with Sheeva.

"Do you like it?" Sheeva asked, pushing the bathroom door open. She stepped into the light, and Fernando realized that she was wearing one of Paris' lacey nightgowns, complete with garters and stockings.

"What the fuck is this?" he asked, sitting up in bed. "Is this a joke or something? What makes you think this is cool?"

"Christ! Not you too!" Sheeva closed the robe around herself and lit a cigarette as she prepared to verbally spar. "Listen, why is it that I can't touch anything of hers, but I have to live with it. Last I checked, I was the only woman of fucking age around here. Are you afraid your daughter is going to bust in here and fight with me over this stupid nightie too?"

"No! She won't get a chance, because you're going to take it the fuck off right now!" Fernando rose from the bed and began to tug at the lacey fabric.

"I can do it myself, asshole!" Sheeva slapped Fernando, causing him to come back to his senses.

"Look, I'm sorry. This just wasn't a good idea. I don't want to be thinking about her when I'm with you. It's too soon"

"You don't want to be thinking about her?" Sheeva gave a mock snicker. "Why the fuck is she everywhere then?" She turned her head in either direction, pointing out all of Paris' left behind treasures. "Here, take her shit and sleep with it tonight! I ain't sleeping in here with you, and damn sure not with your dead wife!"

"Maybe you shouldn't." Fernando drew in a dep breath and rolled over, fighting the urge to pull the discarded lingerie up to his face and see if Sheeva had made Paris' smell disappear.

"I'm serious!" Sheeva warned from the bathroom, where she stood, completely nude, tying her hair in a ponytail. She hoped that the sight of her would cause Fernando to do the gentlemanly thing and beg her to stay, maybe even apologize. "Did you hear me?"

She was about to step into the bedroom again when the shrill sound of the small clock radio on the bathroom counter startled her. Instantly the radio blared Destiny's Child's old song, Nasty girl, a tune that she hadn't heard since owning the CD as a child, some ten or fifteen years earlier. She was certain that no modern radio station should be playing it, especially not the local hip-hop station that she had left the radio tuned to. Having had the large radio in the living room cut on and off by itself so much, she gave the fact that it shouldn't have turned itself on second thought. Still it blared, "Nasty, pout some clothes on I told you. Don't walk out the house without some clothes on, I told you."

"I can't with this shit!" she creamed to the top of her lungs. "Now she's in every one of the radios!"

Fernando was about to argue that she was being silly, even though he knew in his heart that she was exactly right, when he heard another loud scream come from the bathroom. The lights blinked on and off, and the door slammed shut.

Fernando ran towards it and began to jiggle the lock as he heard Sheeva scream one more time. A frying sound echoed through the bathroom, but as the lights flickered once more, Fernando became certain that the frying sound was actually the sound of electricity. He fought harder to break the unyielding door from its hinges. When the door finally gave, Sheeva stood on the edge of the claw-footed tub, her hands touching the ceiling to hold her in place. "She fucking tried to murder me!" she screamed, literally jumping in Fernando's arms. "The goddamn radio sailed across the room, at least two feet, and it landed right in the puddle I had left from washing my hair. If I hadn't jumped up here, I would have been fried like a damn chicken. "

"That's ridiculous!" Fernando tried not to sound insulting. "Maybe you nudged it when you were yelling at me, and you didn't realize…"

"Oh fuck no!" Sheeva took off her engagement ring and tossed it on the bed. "You can't have two wives, Fernando. When you bury the dead one, I might come back."

Chapter 8

Fernando stayed awake all night, even after Sheeva's sister had picked her up, and long after snores drifted from his children's bedrooms. He was thankful to have the day off from work. After a long night of thinking and praying, he had made up his mind that he had to rid the house of Paris, once and for all, no matter how painful removing her things would be. She had chosen to leave them. They didn't have to still live by her rules.

Tears dripped from his face as he started to box up her perfumes and cosmetics. Paris only used the best, which is why her skin was always so flawless and soft to his touch and his touch only. The patrons of the local thrift store would be more than happy to acquire her fifty dollar lotions for as little as half a dollar. He sat on the side of the bed and removed the cap from one of her favorite perfumes, a fragrance that he and the kids had gotten her for her last birthday. Tears came faster as he inhaled the sweet aroma of wild flowers and cotton.

"I'm sorry!" he sobbed, tossing the bottle in the box with the others. "You got to move on now, baby! I miss you, and I will always love you. We all will, but it's time to let you go. You have to leave this house and go where you belong."

A gasp escaped Fernando's throat as a cold breeze brushed past him, so violently that it caused his knees to buckle. He dropped the box of perfumes, but before he had time to lend his attention to the pool of glass and dark liquids that sprawled across the wood floor, he was startled yet again by the sound of every radio in the house turning itself on at once: Nia's boom box, Fernando Jr.'s Karaoke machine, Paris' prized stereo, and even the clock radio in the bathroom (no telling how it managed to survive the electric shock and the brutal toss from the previous night), all blasted Syleena Johnson's "I am your woman."

"NO!" Fernando insisted, running from room to room, trying to turn the music off, to no avail. "Goddamn it, you have to go!" As he bent to unplug Fernando's karaoke machine, a jolt of electricity coursed through his arm, making him shake violently. When it was gone he doubled over to vomit, and his mind was able to focus on the fact that he hadn't even touched the plug when he'd gotten shocked. His hand was at least six inches away from the chord as he struggled to gain the nerve to touch it.

"Goddamn it!" He fell across his son's bed and cried himself to sleep, despite the loud music that blared all around him. As he drifted off, the cold breeze returned, this time much gentler, like a tickle. It seemed to nestle itself around him, caressing him. Though the sweet smell of cotton and wild flowers that accompanied the breeze could have easily been attributed to the shattered bottles of perfume he had left in his bedroom, somehow he knew that his mind was not playing tricks on him. Paris was lying beside him.

His comfort faded as he thought about the danger that her presence posed to his new fiancé, or any other woman that would come into his life. He was afraid to even think the thought in her presence, but he had to find some way to get rid of his dead wife, and very soon.

Chapter 9

"So this is the room that your mother never let me come in?" Maria walked around in circles, trying to pull Fernando Jr.'s attention away from the video game he played on his PC. She rolled the top of her school skirt one more time, just to make it a little shorter. If that, along with the fact that her shirt was completely open, didn't get him to understand that she had not come to soak in his neon posters and rap music, she would have to admit that he was gay, and pony up the five dollars she had bet Kendrid and Sarah.

Fernando was about to answer her in his usual short manner, and turn his attention back to his video game when her lacey bra caught his full attention. "Whoa! What's with thing one and thing two?" he asked, pointing to her chest. He gave a nervous chuckle as she walked closer.

"It's hot in here. Aren't you hot?" Maria spun his chair around. "I think you're hot. I've always thought you were very hot!"

"You do?" Fernando was on the brink of regaining his childhood stutter as he stared at Maria's dark eyes, perfectly circled with makeup and accented with jewels. Though he was not into gothic girls, Maria was the exception.

"You're when cuter when you act al nerdy and clueless." She brushed her hand through his hair and pushed his head back. When her tongue found its way into his mouth, he tried not to shutter, or show any sign that she was giving him his first kiss. His hands fastened around the armrest of the chair, nervous and clumsy.

"Relax." Maria stood and stared at Fernando. Her eyes fell on the growing knot in the front of his pants. She reached out and squeezed it before heading to the door. "I guess I was right, after all."

"Right about what?" Fernando almost grew irate, thinking that Maria was up to her usual teasing.

"Don't worry about it. You'll be glad I was right in about five seconds."

A loud screeching echoed through the room, followed by the sound of electric static. Maria lost her balance on her tall high heel shoes and toppled to the floor as she spun around in fear. The lights flickered violently, and his karaoke machine began to play a song that he recalled his grandparents dancing to in the videos that his mother had shown him when he was younger. He couldn't recall the artist, but he recognized the lyrics, and he also recognized them to mean that his mother was not satisfied with his behavior.

"What in the way of fucks is this shit?!" Maria scurried to her feet and tugged at the doorknob, wondering why Fernando's only reaction to the freak show was laughter.

"It's my mom," he explained calmly. "I told you, she does this. This is her way of keeping us in line." He walked closer to Maria and wrapped his arms around her. "You didn't believe me when I told you all of this last week. Do you see now?"

"This is crazy! You guys just live like this?"

"It's my mom; what should we do; have somebody chase her spirit out?"

"That's exactly what the fuck you should do!" Maria turned to leave again, but a jolt of electricity zapped her, stopping her in her tracks. She began to wail like a baby as the radio flickered again, and the song changed from "Mama used to say" by Junior to "Let's wait a while" by Janet Jackson.

"Okay...okay!" Fernando held back a laugh as he wrapped his arm around Maria's shoulder and ushered her out of his room and towards the front door.

When she was gone, the comfortable familiarity of his mother's lingering spirit changed into fear. Maybe Maria was right. Paris' antics were cool now; maybe even a lifesaver to a fifteen year old boy who was afraid to lose his virginity just yet, but what about in the future? His heart skipped as he thought of his mother scaring every friend he invited over off, maybe even hopping in his karaoke machine and following him off to college, where she would continue to do the same thing. He decided that he would text Nia and his father to call a secret meeting when she returned from soccer practice and his father returned from visiting Sheeva, who was now too afraid to even darken their doorstep.

Chapter 10

"It fucking shocked her!" Fernando Junior stared at his sister, wondering why his story of what had happened to Maria did not move her towards concern. "She could have been killed!"

"She had no business here anyway!" Nia shot back. "Mama is here. Just because she died, doesn't mean she is going to stop being our mother!"

"She tried to electrocute Sheeva the other night," Fernando senior spoke up, rubbing the temples of his head in frustration. "She sent the clock radio flying off the bathroom counter and right into the puddle of shower water Sheeva had left on the floor. It missed her by seconds. If sheeva hadn't seen it coming from the corner of her eye, we might be planning her funeral right now."

"*You* would be planning her funeral!" Nia corrected. "And, again, she does not belong here! I haven't heard anything that mama did to hurt any of *us,* the ones who belong!"

"She tried to hurt me!" Fernando Senior fought back tears, knowing that his daughter would not believe his story. "I was boxing up her stuff, after you guys had gone to school, and she just kept making every radio in the house play the same song louder and louder. I was running around, trying to unplug them, and she shocked the fuck out of me. It knocked me unconscious. Your brother is right, baby. This shit is getting way out of hand!"

"Fine!" Nia rose from the couch and headed towards the door. "Do what you want to do, but while you are busy getting rid of everything that belonged to mama, just so Sheeva can feel safe, remember that I am Mama's child. I might as well go too. I will be t Mrs. Merva's house!"

"Don't even bother!" Fernando Junior grabbed his father's arm, begging him not to chase after his sister. "We have to do this."

"Sheeva has a sister that's into all this witchcraft shit. She says not to touch a thing until she checks the place out. I have been thinking of calling her over here for days now, but I didn't know how you guys would take it."

"We have to do this, Dad. You know it's the right thing. Nia will just have to come around later. This isn't just Mom communicating with us through songs anymore, Dad. Mom is trying to kill people, if *it's* even Mom. I can't imagine Mom ever being cruel to anyone, not even in the afterlife!"

"You're right." Fernando Senior pulled his sweater tighter around him as the air in the room began to get eerily colder. He looked around, sensing that he and his son were not alone in the room. 'Go to Merva and Daryl's tonight! Whatever you do, do not step foot back in this house. If you need me, I'm at Sheeva's sister's. I have a feeling that we pissed Paris…err…what the fuck ever it is, off with all this talk about calling a cleanser in. GO!" He pushed his son towards the door just in time to save him from the borage of CDs that began to fly from the shelf, each twisting in the air before coming towards the men, the sharp corners aimed to draw blood.

"Are you seeing this, Dad?" Fernando Juniors fingers clumsily fumbled with the buttons of his phone, trying to activate his camera. "Holy shit, Dad!"

"Get the fuck out!" Fernando Senior pushed his son out the door as he felt the first of several CDs strike his own back, neck, and the back of his head. "Fuck!" he gasped, looking back through the glass door to see that the CDs continued to fly from the shelf, crashing just in front of the door.

"Nia isn't going to believe this!" Fernando Junior stood on his tiptoes and tried to look over his father's broad shoulders. "I don't know if that's Mom anymore, Dad!"

Chapter 11

"So your shit is really haunted?" Kendrid stared at Fernando Junior in amazement. The fearful look on his friends face made him realize just how serious and scared Fernando was. "Oh shit, man." He stopped toying with his fidget spinner and sat on the edge of the bed, next to his friend. "I do believe you. Maria told me the whole story. Shit is crazy."

"That's the understatement of the year." Fernando yawned and pulled the covers over his nude body. "Anyways, thanks for letting me crash here. Melva and Darryl have enough on their hands with Nia, and my dad is M.I.A., as usual."

"You ever try to get the church to come in and bless the house?" Kendrid blushed as he admired his friend's frame through the thin sheets.

"We never were a church type family." Fernado smiled at Kendrick and adjusted his semi-erection under the sheet. "I know what you're thinking, and the answer is no. You may as well go to your own bed tonight.

"Oh it's like that? You got some play from Maria and now you too straight to kick it with me like we used to?"

"It has nothing to do with you or Maria! I'm just…"

"Scared," Kendrick finished for his friend, as he watched tears form in his eyes. "Look, I know. Look around my room! I took everything digital out, just because I know what you been going through. I aint got no CD player, no Laptop, no alarm clock…none of that shit! I know it's fucked up, and it has to feel even more fucked up that Maria is telling everyone about it, and nobody believes you. I'm here for you. I mean that." Kendrid's arousal subsided as he crawled behind his old friend and wrapped his arms around the trembling boy. "You are safe here. Tonight, you can sleep good."

Fernando silently sobbed as he rubbed the hairs on Kendrick's arm. He intertwined his fingers with Kendrick's silently asking him to stay with him for the rest of the night.

"Whatever it is, it's not your mother." Kendrid stroked Fernando's hair as he spoke. "Ms. Paris didn't have an evil bone in her body, and you know it. Why the hell would she want to torture her kids?"

"I don't know." Fernando was shaking so violently that he fought to get those words out clearly. "It did seem like her, at first, but now, I just don't know. Maybe she decided that she wouldn't put up with all the shit she put up with in the real life in the next one."

"You believe in God; don't you?" Kendrid sat up on one elbow and looked in Fernando's face as he awaited a response. "Well, do you?"

"I guess." Fernando's mind wandered back to earlier that day, when Sarah had stopped him before school and prayed a prayer of protection over him before giving him her grandmother's lucky amulet. She had pointed out that even though he had no strict religious beliefs of his own, having an amulet to protect him could do no harm, after all, he had also never believed in ghosts until the present situation had presented itself. She gave him a kiss on the cheek, which grew into more than her usually friendly kiss. The boy changed positions in bed, remembering the sensation that touching lips with Sarah had caused.

"Well, the bible tells us that God takes the people who were good in life. Your mother is in heaven. Whatever that is at your house is not Ms. Paris."

"I suppose." Fernando didn't know if that thought frightened or calmed him. Of course, he would always want to remember his mother as the good, sweet-natured woman she was, but if she was not the one wreaking havoc on the house, then who was, possibly something or someone who did not share her love of the family, and did not care how far they took hurting people?

"You really like Maria?" Kendrid had regained his erection at the thought of Maria, and had started to sneakily grind himself against Fernando's naked ass as they cuddled.

"She's okay, I guess."

"But are you trying to be with her, or is it cool if I try to holla?"

"Do whatever you want." Fernando scowled, but tried to hide his anger at the fact that the guy he was spooning with had just asked for permission to fuck a girl that he had feelings for. What should it have mattered to him anyway? Sarah had made it clear to him that she had reciprocity for the feelings he had hidden from her since fifth grade. Maria should have been an afterthought. He continued to stroke the hairs on Fernando's arm, also realizing that his mother, or whatever it was, would not be letting him do anything with Maria or Sarah any time soon. "I don't Maria likes you like that, though." The salty part of him allowed him to yawn those words just before drifting off to sleep."

Chapter 12

Fernando Senior parked the car two blocks away from the house. Still shaking, he led Sheeva's sister, Katrina, to towards his yard. He grew more and more annoyed by the woman's energy, even though she had been silent the entire forty-five minute ride. Perhaps that is what bothered him most. When the radio turned on by itself, playing, "And I am telling you," by Jennifer Hudson, the woman sat still, reaching out only to grab his hand and remove it from the radio's dial. Fernando continued driving, though he was near a panic attack. How could Katrina not see that this was a direct warning from Paris? Somehow, she knew that they were going to try to cleanse her from the house. The other part of Fernando felt safe because Katrina did not seem to fear the impending doom.

"You start here," Katrina reached in her bag and handed Fernando a box of salt. "You have to walk backwards, making a line on the property with the salt. This is for cleansing and protection. Don't miss a spot."

"Okay." Fernando nervously opened the box and tried his best to pour the salt in a straight line. Meanwhile, he was being thrown off by Katrina's chanting. He watched her swing a lit bundle of incense from side to side, fanning the smoke with a feather.

Upon meeting Katrina, Fernando instantly pegged her as a quack. She was the complete opposite of her sister, to say the least. Katrina favored corduroy bellbottoms and loud, stretched out, hand knitted sweaters over form fitting designer dresses. Her long, wiry, red hair was pulled to the side with the kind of clips that Fernando remembered his mother and aunts wearing in the late seventies and early eighties. The freakish ensemble was completed with a pair of black cat-eyed glasses. The fact that she rubbed him down from head to toe with several crystals before allowing him to enter he meek trailer didn't help to sway his opinion of her lunacy, but he needed help badly, and Sheeva seemed convinced that her nut-job of a sister was the answer.

"I feel an energy," Katrina whispered. She held up her finger to warn Fernando to not approach her as she stood still with her eyes closed, and began to chant in some language that was neither Spanish nor English.

Hearing her do so also did nothing to curb Fernando's hunch that she was crazy, or either Sheeva was playing an elaborate joke on him, but he knew that the second reckoning couldn't be true, because Sheeva was also into spirituality, and took such things serious. He also knew that she was equally concerned for the safety of him and his kids.

"Have you completed the barrier?" Katrina seemed almost normal as she turned to Fernando and asked those words. "You have to make sure that you have left no open spaces, no matter how small they appear to you, they are big enough to invite an unwanted guest. This is for our safety!"

"I understand." Fernando shook his head as he walked halfway around the property, checking to make sure he had sealed it off completely. "It's done."

"We can enter now." Katrina motioned for Fernando to unlock the front door, which he did with hands so shaky that he had to attempt putting the key in the door at least five times before getting the job done.

When they were inside, Fernando's eyes bulged and his heart banged away at the walls of his chest. He turned to face Katrina, but no words would come out of his mouth as he attempted to speak. He pointed to the neatly re-stacked CD tower. "This… can't be!" he stammered. He began to tremble as he fought to tell Katrina that no one had been in the house since the violent episode that he and Fernando Jr. had suffered three days earlier. After locking the house up, he had taken the extra keys from both of his children to make sure they did not return to the unsafe environment. He had even made up a story about needing the spare key he had given Daryl and Merva back to ensure their safety.

Katrina nodded her head, showing that she totally believed him; why else would she have come? Her dark eyes glistened behind her cat-glasses as she tugged at her crystal and outstretched one arm, moving her fingers about as if she were trying to touch something tangible. "She's trying to hide from me." Those words were spoken with a slight grin, which implied that Paris would not be successful in her attempts.

Fernando stood at the door, still clutching his chest as he tried to decide whether or not Katrina's cockiness should soothe him. Paris' recent attacks on him, Sheeva, and even her own son, had made him fearful of what she was capable of. Those were the beginning warnings. The song in the car, and the way he had to fight to keep the stirring wheel from jerking each time they passed a large truck, made it clear to Fernando that Paris would not be easily thrown out of her own home, one which she had payed half off on her own, working as a teacher's assistant, and then a nurse, while he finished his degree in physics. After betraying her the way he had, he felt bad about even trying to cleanse her spirit from the house. If the spirit in the house was actually Paris, and if she was evil now, it was totally because of his infidelity and the ungratefulness of the children.

Katrina nearly jumped out of her skin, and Fernando scooted backwards, wrenching his body the entire two feet distance out of the door he had been sanding wait at when the radio turned itself on. This time, Miranda Lambert's "Gunpowder and lead" blared from Paris' unplugged stereo system: "You want a fight, well boy you got one, and he ain't seen me crazy yet," the country songstress sang, expressing Paris' warning.

"Don't!" Katrina warned as she noticed Fernando about to leap into a full run. "This is your house, and you have to take it back. You can't have any fear. Besides, you can't leave the circle of salt we've made until the place is cleansed. If you do, you will never get rid of whatever this is!" She reached into her bag and handed Fernando a paper that had words he could hardly pronounce scribbled in a scratchy handwriting. He was also given a spritz bottle. "Holy water and pure salt," she explained. "When you feel threatened, say the words on that paper, and spray the water in the direction you feel the threat coming from."

"I'm not sure I have enough." Fernando tried to force a laugh as he followed Katrina down the hall. Lights flickered, and the radio blared, though the song became nearly inaudible due to the static interference.

"IT's trying to communicate!" Katrina warned. "IT's going to try to sound like your wife. Don't listen to it, and don't speak back to it! Whatever it says to you, concentrate on saying the prayer I gave you, and when you feel it close, spray the water!"

Fernando stopped in his tracks as he heard what appeared to be Paris' voice, faintly calling his name through the loud static. He continued on, as Katrina gave him a warning nudge. Sweat poured from his face so profusely that he could barely make out the writing on the paper, but he fought with all he had inside of him to comply with Katrina, who walked throughout the house, fanning sage smoke and chanting words he had never heard.

As he had been directed, Fernando made sure that every window and door to the house had been left open after being smudged by Katrina. When the house was so smoky that they could barely make out each other's images, the radio stopped playing. He stared at Katrina, awaiting further direction.

They both jumped as a high pitched wail of pain came from the stereo. It faded away gradually as the dials on the old machine flickered and then their light also faded. A cold breeze violently brushed past them, blowing out the white candle that Katrina had set in the middle of the floor.

"It has left." Katrina smiled as she stared into Fernando's worried face. "It's gone now. Didn't you feel it leave?"

Fernando looked around the house, as if he knew what to look for in the first place, and then he breathed in a sigh of relief, noticing that the heavy tension he had felt lately had dissipated. He grabbed his future sister in law into a hug and spun her around as he danced with jubilation. "IT's over!" he rejoiced, literally jumping halfway to the ceiling. "It's over!"

"And you and Sheeva can move back in and replace all the bad memories with good ones." Katrina gave him a playful nudge in the shoulder. "It really is over, Fernando!" she promised him. "It can only comeback if you or your kids invite it back. I'm going to give you something to make sure you keep that from happening." She withdrew a yellow stone from her bag and gave it to him, instructing him to place it just beneath the front door once every member of the household had crossed the threshold again.

"Sure." He half-smiled as he placed the stone in his pocket. "Thanks for everything. Tell your sister to be ready tonight. I'm going to pick my kids up from school, and after we have our family time, I'll pick her up for our usual date night."

"You'd better bring me a doggy bag!" Katrina teased, heading for her car. "By the way, it's a conduit." She stopped in the doorway and pointed to the radio. "Yeah, now that one spirit used it to come through, it's pretty much an open portal. Get rid of it!"

"You don't have to tell me twice!" Fernando moved to the far end of the large stereo and began to inch it towards the door with his arms and hip. His heart nearly broke as he thought of how distraught Nia would be when she discovered the last piece of her mother had been sat out to the curb for trash. "Oh well!" he said aloud, continuing to follow Katrina's order.

Chapter 13

Fernando Senior fought to make himself choke down the plate of seasoned curly fries and the overstuffed burger that sat before him. Though the length of time seemed like an eternity since he could last recall when he was able to taste anything, and his stomach bubbled with nervous gas from missing many meals, he pushed the fries around on his plate, and stared at his daughter, who wore her usual scowl of anger. 'What?" he asked, gently grabbing her arm as he noticed that she mimicked his action of scattering her food around on her plate.

"It's not fair!" she blurted out. "This is supposed to be family night! How come Fernando got to bring Sarah along? You even had the common sense to tell Sheeva not to come!"

"Fernando has known Sarah most of his life. She is very much like family to him, and if you notice their interaction, soon she will be like family to you." Fernando Senior smiled at his daughter as he pointed to his son, dancing close with his childhood acquaintance.

"She sat where Mom usually sits!" Nia shoved her plate away in annoyance and her voice was raised in protest. "I like Sarah, but I don't like *this*!" she said through gritted teeth, as she pointed to the vacated chair to her right. "Nobody can take Mom's place!"

"So that's what this is all about?" Fernando Senior breathed a sigh of relief as he realized that Nia was actually behaving very normal for a child who had lost a parent. He scooted towards her in the booth and was about to wrap his arm around her shoulders when the sound of one of Paris' favorite songs thundered from the jukebox and filled the restaurant. The nervous man nearly jumped out of his skin. He knocked his soda over as his protruding eyes scanned the restaurant.

A young girl, with rainbow-colored weave, gave him a strange look as his eyes settled upon her. She gave a faint smile and then returned her attention to feeding quarters into the juke box.

"You thought it was *her*, huh?" Nia giggled and drained her cherry coke as she enjoyed the look of fright on her father's face. She watched her brother and Sarah twirl in circles as "Cater to you" by Destiny's Child echoed through the restaurant. "I bet he marries her before you marry Sheeva," she joked, stealing a pickle from her father's plate. "At least, their marriage will last longer. They actually know one another."

"Maybe." Fernando forced himself to choke back the anger inside as he stared at his daughter's smug grin. "How did someone so small get all this insight?"

"Mama always said I have an old soul." Nia winked, as her mother often would do before sharing an inside joke.

Fernando Senior could not decide why, but that one innocent action from his child made every hair on his back stand on edge. He waved his hand to signal to the dancing couple that he was ready to get the hell out of the establishment.

The two teens smiled and held hands as they approached Nia and Fernando senior. Fernando Junior's eyes widened, mimicking the fear in his father's eyes as he got closer. "What?" he asked his clearly flustered father. "Come on, Dad! What is it?"

Just as Fernando senior opened his mouth to speak, the juke box cut the current song short, and "Never gonna let you go," by Tina Moore enveloped the restaurant. He nervously reached for his wallet and stacked three twenty dollar bills on the table as he ushered his kids towards the door.

On the way out, the young girl, who had fed the juke box quarters earlier was in a heated argument with the manager, demanding to be compensated because the faulty jukebox had played a song that she had not selected. Fernando's Senior tried to remain calm as he processed the fact that the song played on the radio was nearly thirty years old, and no doubt, not even a choice on the juke box, which had been stacked with hits from the late 2000's as long as he could recall.

"Sir, do I look like anybody who got to lie to get fifty cents from your ass?!" the girl questioned, showcasing her arm full of gold and diamond jewelry. "I picked out three of my girlfriend's favorite song, 'cause I was working my way up to proposing to her! You don't know how bad this shit fucked me up, sir! I ain't never heard this shit here before in all my life, sir!"

Fernando Senior stopped in his tracks and wrestled inside his pocket. He pulled out a crumpled five dollar bill and nervously handed it to the angry young lady. "My kids were over there. They may have accidently done something to the jukebox. Sorry for any trouble they caused."

"Thank you, Mister!" the girl gave a cherub-like smile as she accepted the crumpled bill and looked over her shoulder to roll her eyes at the blushing manager. 'I knew something had to have happened, 'cause I damn sure don't have to try to cheat anybody out of fifty-fucken-cents!"

"Good luck with your proposal." Fernando gave both the girl and the manager an apologetic nod as he rushed out the door to join his kids in the car.

"You said it was over!" Fernando Junior said accusingly. "It's not is it? That weird song back there was her, huh?"

"Calmamente, por favor!" Fernando Senior screamed, banging against the stirring wheel with his fists.

Nia and Fernando settled back in their seats, recalling that their father only used his native, Spanish tongue when angered beyond reason.

"I think I'll walk home." Sarah gave Fernando a kiss on the cheek and wrestled her arm free as he begged her to stay in the car. "No! This is a family affair. You work this out, and I will see you at school tomorrow."

"Okay." Fernando Junior bit back his own anger as he watched his girlfriend jog towards the diner. "She's never gonna let us go, is she?" A tear slid down his face as he punched the seat in front of him. "Just like that song kept saying on the restaurant, she's never gonna let us go!"

"Your mother is gone!" Fernando senior yelled, cranking the car up and pulling unto the freeway. "I don't want to hear anything else about your mother. She made her choice!"

"Tell *her* that!" Fernando Junior's voice trembled with fear as her pointed to the untouched radio dials, which lit up and scanned for a station.

Nia remained unbothered, drawing pictures on the fogged up windows, as she had done every trip, since she was a small child.

When the radio settled on a station, Faith Evans' "Never let you go" played, louder than any of them had ever heard the ragged car radio go before.

A smile came to Nia's face as she began to hum along to the lyrics. She stopped drawing and stared ahead of her, etheric ally.

"Stop that!" Fernando Junior begged, shaking his sister. "Turn it off, Dad!" he insisted, though he knew his request was impossible.

Fernando Senior's face boiled with sweat as he fought to keep the stirring wheel from being yanked away by some unseen force. He tried not to alarm his children of the danger. His heart danced around in his chest cavity as he recalled that he had parked the car far away from the house before drawing the circle of salt for Katrina's ritual. Paris had left the house and could not return, but she had attached herself to the trusty old, family Honda. Even the stone in his pocket couldn't protect them now.

Once the song had ended and started to reply a second time, Fernando Junior gave up his panic. Fighting the inevitable was useless. He settled back in his chair and tears streamed from his eyes as he took Nia's hand into his and joined his sister in singing the melody of the song.

Fernando Senior still fought to regain control of the car, silently saying every prayer he had learned in catholic school. Just as they neared the path that turned into their neighborhood, the unseen force snatched the wheel harder than ever, sending the car cascading into the path of a speeding sixteen wheeler.

Only Fernando Senior screamed. The children continued to sing along with their mother's chosen song until they could be heard no more.

The End